ROGUE FOR HIRE

A Regency Historical Romance

ROGUES OF THE ROAD

SASHA COTTMAN

Copyright © 2021 by Sasha Cottman

All rights reserved.

No part of this book may be reproduced in any form or by any electronic or mechanical means, including information storage and retrieval systems, without written permission from the author, except for the use of brief quotations in a book review.

Prologue

Lord Harry Steele hauled his trunk into the stable yard of the coaching company, and with a tired sigh, dumped it against the nearest wall. He had managed to get it this far without breaking his back, but every muscle in his body was screaming—not to mention the sweat and stench of stale booze which oozed from his every pore.

His coat was dirty and torn. The whereabouts of his best hat a mystery for the ages. He looked more like a rag-and-bone man than the son of the Duke of Redditch.

Why do dukes have to be so bloody stubborn? He could have at least offered me the use of the coach.

Slowly catching his breath, he took the time to survey his surroundings. The view pained his already disappointed heart. Grimy, dull, grey brick walls rose on all sides of the square. The only coach in the yard had two wheels missing and looked like it had seen better days. There was a noticeable lack of clean hay and stable staff. If the place had once been well-maintained, it wasn't any time this century.

Please lord, don't let this be where the last of my pennies have gone.

Harry pulled a piece of paper out of his pocket and checked the address.

82 Gracechurch Street, London

He sighed. Miracles were definitely in short supply this morning.

A quick check of the stables revealed three horses, but again, no hay or stable hands. The only positive thing was that the mounts meant that some of his fellow RR Coaching Company investors had arrived.

"Well, I hope one of them has deep pockets, because this is going to be a black hole of money," he muttered.

He made his way out to the yard once more, regretting yet again his decision to give the whisky a serious nudge the previous evening. It was bad enough to be penniless and homeless; a hangover just added insult to injury.

"Harry, get your useless arse upstairs. We are waiting for you," cried a voice.

Lifting his head, his gaze settled on a tall figure at the top of a nearby set of wooden steps. He gave a tired wave. Lord Andrew McNeal, the Duke of Monsale; stood with hands on hips glaring at him from his lofty perch.

"Coming," said Harry, and he headed toward the stairs. When his tired legs finally got him to the landing, Harry offered a bow. "Your grace."

Monsale sniffed, then pointed at Harry's trunk abandoned in the yard. "I take it the old man made good on his threat."

"Two days out from Christmas Eve, and he tosses me into the street. What sort of father does that, I ask you?" replied Harry.

"One whom you have pushed to the limits of his good humor from the day you first drew breath?" offered Monsale.

He couldn't expect sympathy from his friends. They knew all the wicked things Harry had got up to over the years, including the ones which had escaped his father's notice.

"I know, but this is Christmas. I didn't think he would do it, let alone during the festive season," said Harry.

And who is going to get all that lovely pork crackling and roast beef on Christmas Eve? Not to mention the sweet Brussels sprouts. Not me.

Being excluded from the grand family dinner was the biggest blow of them all. He could just taste the thick, rich gravy as it drowned his peas and carrots.

"It is done, and no amount of grizzling will do you any good. Come on. We have work to do," said Monsale. He put a comforting arm around Harry's shoulder and ushered him through a nearby door.

"Good Prince Hal!" came the cry.

Harry chuckled. If he had a penny for every time Shakespeare had been quoted at him, he wouldn't be in this mess. As it was, he was closer to a pauper than a prince this morning, but it was still comforting to know that his friends considered him worthy of their jests.

Seated at a long, grime-covered table were three other men. Sir Stephen Moore, Augustus Trajan Jones, and The Honorable George Hawkins. None of them seemed the least fazed by Harry's disheveled appearance.

Monsale walked over to Augustus Jones and held out his hand. "Pay up, Gus. The old man finally did it."

Gus's mouth opened as wide as a trout caught on a hook. "Oh well, it's taken ten long years for me to have to pay out the bet, so I consider it money well spent."

With a flourish, he handed over a pound note, which Monsale quickly perused before putting into his own pocket. No one remarked over the sight of a duke checking his friend's money for any possible signs of forgery. Only a fool took a banknote on face value.

Sir Stephen Moore waved a hip flask in Harry's direction, and Harry took it without hesitation. This morning called for the hair of the dog.

Harry dropped into the empty, dusty chair between Stephen and George, and downed a large mouthful of whisky.

"Right, now that we are all here, let's get the inaugural meeting of the RR Coaching Company underway," said Monsale.

"RR Coaching Company?" replied Gus.

Harry grinned. It had been his idea to call their new and barely legal endeavor after an old moniker which his father had attached to him and his friends.

"We could hardly openly call ourselves the Rogues of the Road Coaching Company," said Monsale.

The tatty old stables and grounds of what had once been a successful coaching business would be the perfect front for their new enterprise.

Monsale nodded. "Harry?"

Harry put down the hip flask and got to his feet. He might well be the one with the least amount of money in his pocket, but this plan had been spinning around in his head for several years.

He cleared his throat. "If this was a formal company meeting, someone would be taking minutes, but I expect none of us want anything we discuss to be put in writing. Firstly, may I thank you all for investing your hard-earned blunt in this venture. I know most of us don't have more than one or two pennies to rub together."

He gave a quick sideways glance at Monsale. The Duke of Monsale was wealthy, but also tightfisted with his coin. His parsimonious nature was evident in the state of the premises he had secured for the group's new venture.

"And while the current state of this place is not going to give Carlton House a run for its money, it will, however, furnish us with a front for our less reputable activities until we can get the coaching service properly established."

While Monsale helped to provide a respectable façade to the fledgling coaching business, the rest of the group would continue to fund its development by way of their secret business dealings. Gus smuggled goods into Britain on board his yacht, the *Night Wind*. George helped to find new homes for items of dubious ownership. And Stephen had dealings in the murky world of revenge and personal vendettas.

He didn't need to give voice to what they all were likely thinking. At some point in the future, a crisis would occur, and they would have to find a respectable way to earn money. But that day was not today. The RR Coaching Company was their safe retreat for the time being.

Harry dusted the front of his coat but didn't bother making too much of an effort. There was every chance he would be sleeping on the floor of this place tonight, or in the stables.

"And what will be my contribution to the RR Coaching Company, you quietly ask yourself? Well, London society thinks it knows everything about my scandalous lifestyle, but in truth, I have only ever allowed a tiny portion of it to become public. I pride myself on being able to manage my image. So, I have decided that instead of creating scandals, I am going to get other people to pay me in order to make theirs go away."

He was going into the dirty-deeds business.

Monsale clapped his hands. "Lord Harry Steele, the man who knows scandals better than anyone. I shall personally recommend you to all my friends who need their naughty secrets kept."

Harry would maintain his personae of 'society wild boy,' while at the same time taking on clients who had got themselves into a spot of serious trouble and who would gladly pay for his expertise. Who better to keep a lid on the bubbling scandals of the *ton* than someone who not only understood

London society, but who had seen its wicked, sinful underbelly?

His other friends joined in the applause.

Stephen patted him on the back. "Harry, you are a genius."

Harry grinned. "Was there ever any doubt?"

Chapter One

※※※

E*leven months later*

Alice North stood out the front of number 16 Grosvenor Street, London, and quietly swore under her breath. "How the bloody hell has it come to this?"

In her hand, she held a small card. She glanced at it, still uncertain as to whether she was doing the right thing.

Scandals managed. Secrets kept. Cash retainer required. Instalments as per contract.

16 Grosvenor Street, London

What kind of man would run a business which specialized in such matters? If the twenty-page nondisclosure agreement she had been made to sign before receiving the business card was any indication, more than likely, he was the wrong sort.

She turned, mind half made up to get back into the carriage and head home, but the thought of her sister stopped her. Alice was fast running out of options, and if she didn't do something soon, all could be lost.

"Come on. Let's have you," she muttered.

She let out a long, slow breath, and considered the front of the house once more. It was an elegant, cream-fronted Georgian-period establishment. The generous width of the house afforded it five window bays and . . .

"Oh, for heaven's sake, stop worrying about the architecture, and go knock on the door!"

A hurried glance around showed no one to be within hearing distance of her, but the fact that she was talking to herself had Alice fearing for her sanity.

An extremely tall, solidly built man dressed all in black answered the door, and Alice's heart immediately sank. Had there been a death in the family? The way her luck was running this morning, it wouldn't surprise her in the least if she had turned up at the exact same time as the undertaker.

"Yes." He looked at Alice down the length of his nose as he spoke.

She scowled. That was not the usual way for a servant to address a visitor. The man's demeanor bordered on rude. "I. Hmm. I came about . . . oh," she stammered.

I knew this was a stupid idea.

The man held out a hand, clicking his fingers impatiently at her. "Do you have a card?" he snapped.

Without thinking, Alice offered him the simple white card she had been holding onto with grim determination since leaving home a short while earlier.

The butler took one look at the card and loudly sighed. "I meant *your* card."

She fumbled in her reticule as heat raced to her cheeks. Where was a card case when you needed it in a hurry?

"Ah," she said, and pulled out her calling card.

He took it, barely glanced at it, and with a disinterested wave, beckoned Alice into the house. She gritted her teeth, fighting the temptation to call him out on his impertinence. Her mother most certainly would have done so and then had words with his employer.

"Thank you," she said.

Why am I thanking this man?

The door was closed, and without another word, the butler promptly turned on his heel and headed upstairs, abandoning Alice in the foyer.

She softly tutted to herself. "What a morning."

Doing her best to calm her temper, Alice took in the downstairs area. It was nothing to write home about. Plain black and white checkered tiles. The walls were painted cream and unadorned. It could have been the entrance to any one of a hundred other homes in London. The resident of this house clearly didn't care for adding any personal touches.

She waited.

The butler hadn't even offered for her to sit somewhere.

And she waited.

I wonder what the cook has planned for luncheon today. I am famished.

She was humming a tune softly to herself when the butler finally reappeared at the top of the stairs. He made his way to her in an unhurried fashion. Alice bit back a remark about his lack of manners. Now was not the time to take the man to task.

"His lordship is ready to receive you," he announced.

Lordship? When did things get so bad that nobles had to take up paid employment?

Upstairs, Alice was shown into a drawing room and *finally* offered a seat. With as much grace as her tired feet would permit, she settled into an overstuffed purple sofa. The cushions were so soft that she immediately sank into them, leaving her lying prone, staring at the ceiling.

Ruddy hell, this is ridiculous. I really shouldn't have come here.

She waited until the butler had left the room before struggling out of her pillowed prison and getting to her feet. She gave the sofa a disapproving look then headed over to the window. The curtains were closed and the room poorly lit.

It's eleven o'clock. Who keeps the drapes drawn at this hour?

How anyone expected to conduct business in such a strange room was beyond her.

Taking one of the deep red sashes in hand, she pulled it back and hung it over a window hook. She reached for the other curtain.

This rogue had better be worth every penny that I've given him. She was already regretting having bothered to wait, fearing this was not going to help her cause in the least.

"Ow! Ow! What the devil are you doing? Are you trying to kill me?"

She whirled round and her gaze fell on a dark-haired man standing a yard or so away. He had moved so silently; she hadn't heard him enter the room and come up behind her.

His left hand was held to his face, covering his eyes. Alice suspected that the only reason he hadn't put both hands to his face was because of the small piglet he had tucked under his right arm.

Not for the first time this morning, Alice found herself scowling at a male of the species. A man who was adorned in a yellow-and-green-floral dressing gown. This house seemed inhabited by the most peculiar of men. And pigs.

The piglet gave her a friendly snort, instantly winning the most-welcoming-member-of-the-household award.

Why is he holding a pig?

"The window. Sunlight. Woman, have you no sense of pity for a man in pain?"

"What you do mean you are in pain?" she replied, her gaze moving from the animal to its outrageously dressed owner.

With a huff, he pushed past her and took a hold of the drape. She sensed he was about to let it fall back and cover the window, but to her surprise, he didn't.

He gripped the curtain tightly in his hand, then let out a tired sigh. "You obviously have never suffered from a hangover, and therefore have no understanding of the hell that one is. I shall give you the grace of your lack of knowledge, but only this one time."

"Thank you. I think," she replied.

Why am I thanking people who are unconscionably rude to me?

This so-called lord clearly hadn't bothered to suffer through any sort of instruction as to how one should behave in the company of a lady. His education in that sphere was sadly lacking. Alice had a sudden inkling as to where his butler had gotten his prickly sense of self-worth from.

Patience. This is more important than your pride. Remember what is at stake.

There was an awkward moment of silence, during which time their gazes were locked in a silent battle. Alice determinedly stared the outrageously dressed hungover fool down. He was not going to get the better of her.

The task was, however, made a little easier by the wonder of his light-green eyes. They held all the promise of a lush meadow on a summer's day. Well, except for the red rim around the edges that did him no favors.

He finally looked at the pig, softly chuckling while he gave the animal a friendly pat. Bending, he set the piglet gently on the floor and it scampered away.

"Lord Harry Steele at your service. Miss . . . what was your bloody name again?" he asked, thrusting out a hand.

"Miss Alice North," she ground out.

Lord Harry Steele? Oh no, I've heard of him. He is a scandalous disgrace.

Little wonder the contract she had signed hadn't mentioned him specifically by name—rather it had only referred to him as being the party of the first and her as the party of the second.

I am an utter fool.

Alice took a hold of his offered appendage and gave it a hard squeeze. If nothing else, this pompous ass would remember her when she was gone. She was already making plans to forget this morning.

What a pity it was him. There goes that small ray of hope. Now I will have to look for another way to deal with this mess.

Lord Steele was busily wincing over his crushed fingers and barely managed a nod in response. When Alice finally released him from her vise-like grip, he studied his hand.

"That's a good shake you have there, Miss North. Remind me not to get on your bad side," he said.

Alice finally saw an opening. "Actually, you are already in my black book. Your butler is unbelievably rude, and you, Lord Steele, have a good deal of my money."

All humor disappeared from his face. Her father was big in trade and always talked about the 'aha' moment in contract negotiations. The point where the other party finally understood that you were deadly serious and were done with bandying words and dealing.

Money always speaks loudest.

"You have paid me a retainer?" he replied.

"Yes. And to use your uncouth language, a bloody big one. I came here today because apart from receiving your business card, I haven't heard a thing since my footman delivered the money and the signed contract to number eighty-two Gracechurch Street three days ago."

He raised an eyebrow. "Impatient little minx, aren't you?"

"Say what you want, Lord Steele, but time is not something I have in abundance," she bit back.

He winced. "Oh, no. Please don't tell me you are pregnant."

Alice's eyes went wide and her mouth fell open in shock. "What? How dare you. I mean, you . . ."

He waved her protests away as if asking an unmarried woman about an inconvenient pregnancy was something, he did every other day. She had a horrid feeling that it probably was.

"Good. Though if you were knocked up, I would have expected you to have dissolved into tears the second you laid eyes on me. Believe me, Miss North, I can deal with most scandals, but unwanted by-blows are the worst. I cannot begin to tell you how many times I have had to hold a pistol to the head of a reluctant father-to-be in order to convince him of the need for a speedy wedding," he replied.

"Lord Steele, I assure you I am not in the family way," she replied.

"Harry. Only those trying to curry favor with my father call me Lord Steele. Not that it does them any good. I couldn't be further from the Duke of Redditch's purse if I tried."

His father was a duke and yet he was handling people's scandals for money; what sort of reprobate had she given her precious funds over to?

Harry stepped forward and took hold of Alice's hand. He slipped the glove from her fingers, then bent and placed a soft, warm kiss on her fingertips. A shiver raced down her spine.

"I have come about my sister, Patience. I am certain I made that clear in the note I sent along with the money and paperwork," she said, trying to maintain her focus.

When he lifted his head and their gazes met once more, he gave her a gentle smile. "My apologies. While I may appear to be a tad flippant, I can assure you that I looked into your case. The fact that you have my card with my home address on it proves that I am serious about this matter. These things often take a little time at the outset, hence my lack of communication."

I don't suppose you getting blind drunk had anything to do with it. What have I signed myself up for?

With a flourish, he handed her the glove. "Now, I have it on good authority that you will be at Viscount and Lady Ashton's ball this evening, as will your darling sister, Patience," he announced.

His words left her stunned. The decision to attend the ball had only been made late the previous evening, the formal RSVP having been sent just before Alice left home.

"How on earth did you discover our plans for tonight?" she asked.

Who is this Lord Harry Steele?

She got the merest hint of a raised eyebrow in response to her question. Alice found herself challenging her first take on him. For all his eccentric behavior, it would appear that there was a good deal more to this man than floral garments and piglets.

"I shall be at the ball tonight. I need to observe your sister and this blackguard in action."

"But you don't know that Cuthbert Saint will be in attendance," she replied.

"If he is the sort of man, I suspect he is, Miss North, he won't waste the opportunity. Until then." He released her hand and stepped back.

Alice stood dumbfounded as Harry bent at the waist, bowed to her, then righted himself and walked straight out of the room.

He called to the piglet as he left. "Come, Milton. Let us seek our breakfast."

Alice was still pondering the events of the past half hour when the butler reappeared and announced that her audience with Lord Steele was at an end.

Once downstairs, he opened the front door and gently pushed her out into Grosvenor Street. As he put his hand on the small of her back, he leaned in. "Next time send a footman ahead and announce your visit. There's a good girl."

Alice went to protest his outright rudeness but found the door swiftly and most firmly shut behind her.

She headed toward the waiting North family carriage, the weight of the world on her shoulders. The temptation to break down and cry was there, but she stubbornly resisted.

Lord Harry Steele had been her last faint hope to save her sister from the clutches of an unashamed fortune hunter.

Damn. Blast. And double bloody . . .

But instead of meeting a mystery man of the world who would give her valuable advice and guidance, she had spent five minutes with London's foremost peacock. Someone with a reputation as a drunkard and a dandy—a cautionary tale. A man whose own father had apparently disowned him.

And yet he knew you were going to the Ashtons' ball tonight.

After climbing into the carriage, Alice found herself looking out the window and staring at the second floor of number sixteen. She caught a glimpse of Harry framed by the red drapes. He gave her a wave.

The man was odd, unashamedly rude, but also fascinatingly attractive. Especially those green eyes. There was something special about Harry Steele.

As the carriage pulled out into the street, Alice's gaze remained fixed on the house. Could he be the answer to her prayers?

I have a horrid feeling I may come to regret this, but I am beyond desperate.

The truth was, as long as Lord Harry Steele was better at managing scandals than he was at choosing his attire, she didn't particularly care how he went about things.

If Harry could save her sister, Alice would follow him to the gates of hell.

Chapter Two

❧

Harry finished off the last of his smoked salmon and pushed back from the table. Breakfast was always his favorite meal of the day. There was nothing better to settle his stomach and throbbing head than a hearty plate of food.

He rose, leaving Milton to finish his own platter of vegetables and softened grains on the floor of dining room. People may say what they wanted about pigs, but Harry had often found them to be in possession of better table manners than many of his peers. And they were most studious about being clean.

After heading to the main drawing room, feeling slightly more human, he opened the rest of the curtains and let the late morning sun into the room. He tied the drapes back and tidied the ends.

It was early December, and any hours where sunshine warmed the house were welcome. Winter was fast closing in and soon it would be dark days and biting cold. Harry loathed winter.

Sir Stephen Moore was lounging on the purple sofa, his head back, eyes partially closed. "You really do make a fetching housemaid. Let me know when you are going to clean out the fire grate. It could be entertaining."

Harry gave the cold, dead fire one resigned look and sighed. The housekeeper only came every other morning, which meant that unless he got on his knees and cleaned out the fire, he would have to suffer a chilly house for the rest of the day.

At least Cook comes each day to feed us.

"Yes, well, you didn't help my financial situation by playing the uptight, rod-up-his-arse butler. You are supposed to be gracious and polite to my clients, not treat them like last week's smelly fish. Leaving Miss North in the foyer was beneath even you," said Harry.

Harry would dearly love a small retinue of servants. Or at least enough money in his bank account to be able to consider employing one or two on a full-time basis.

All his hard-earned coin currently went into the upkeep of the house and paying for his share of the coaching business which he, along with Stephen and the others, were still trying to get established.

He glanced at his dressing gown and frowned. Fashion was his only real vice. It was also the perfect cover for his money-making endeavors. Few people, other than his closest friends and some of his clients, knew the truth of what lay hidden behind Harry's outrageous peacock act.

And since all his clients had their own dirty little scandals which they badly wanted kept hidden, there was little to no risk of anyone daring to spill Harry's or anyone else's secrets to the world. London society was a cesspit of wicked behavior and double standards.

Stephen sat up in the chair as Milton trotted into the room and made a beeline for the sofa. He scooped up the piglet and placed him in a sunny spot on a cushion. "So, what did your pretty little client want? Whatever it is, she must be desperate. She stuck around even after I left her standing in the foyer."

Yes, she was rather fetching, come to think of it.

Her pale blonde hair had matched her dark lemon gown perfectly. Not to mention those hazel eyes which had held his gaze and challenged him. She intrigued him. Not many women did.

"What did she want? The usual. A family scandal that needs to be managed before it gets legs. A younger sister in peril," Harry replied.

She hadn't held back on him. Alice North was not going to be one of those clients who merely handed over money and then didn't want to know anything else until the job was done. He was going to be held accountable by the tempting chit.

This could be a fun challenge. She is more than pretty; the girl has spine. Dare I say, a certain je ne sais quoi.

He made a mental note to keep Stephen as far away from Alice as possible. If anyone was going to form a bond with her, it would be him. Mixing business with pleasure was always risky, but there was something about Miss North which had him intrigued. Tempted even.

I wonder what Miss North will be wearing this evening. One could hope for something daring. Those breasts of hers could look a wonder in a tight bodice.

But if Harry knew anything, he knew people. If Alice was playing the role of big sister and doing her all to defend her younger sibling, she wouldn't dare come to a major social event in anything that drew attention. He would have a pound bet on Miss North wearing a plain gown, possibly cream. Something that would allow her to blend in with the crowd.

He crossed the lushly carpeted drawing room to his writing desk. He wasn't one for having a separate formal study; those rooms reminded him too much of his stiff, stoic father. And extra rooms had to be heated. Anywhere that he could save a coin was worth it. Paying his share of the RR Coaching Company seed money was a constant battle.

"Miss Alice North has a sister. Patience is her name, but apparently not her virtue. From what I understand, she has fallen under the spell of a money-hungry blackguard whom her sister fears will talk her into eloping with him," said Harry.

When Stephen sighed, Harry slowly nodded. People were such clichés.

"I know. Eloping to Gretna Green is so passé. Dare one say it borders on gauche," he added.

On the sofa, a contented Milton rolled over and presented his belly to Stephen, who began to gently rub the soft bristles on the piglet's skin. Little oinks hummed in the room.

"What happened to making the effort to get in an old man's favor? Chaps these days are far too eager to turn their horses' heads north and make for Scotland rather than endure endless meetings with their future fathers-in-law," said Stephen.

"Yes, well, it is the fashion. Quick and easy. But even if this unscrupulous beast Cuthbert Saint makes it all the way to the border with the younger North sister, he won't find anyone willing to perform the marriage service for them," he replied.

He pulled out a plain brown folio and opened it. He perused it for a moment, before closing it again. At this early stage of the contract, he had little information to work with, but he had put in place the usual measures.

After receiving instructions from Alice North, along with his retainer, the first thing Harry had done was to send his own man to Gretna Green in Scotland. A handful of bribes would ensure that Miss Patience North and her prospective groom wouldn't be able to wed if they sought to marry outside the rules of English law.

"It may sound callous of me, but isn't the North family

new money? I mean, sometimes these people don't seem to understand how polite society works. Take how your client arrived this morning; I can't imagine your sister or mine, if I had one, being allowed to wander the streets of London without at least a maid and a burly footman in tow," said Stephen.

"Yes, Gordon North made his money in textiles and shipping. Damn near as rich as Croesus if any of the rumors are to be believed," replied Harry.

Though his friend did have a point about the behavior of Miss Alice North. What business did she have in calling on someone like him without at least a chaperone? From where he came, it simply wouldn't stand. Young women of rank and high birth wouldn't dare do such a thing. His sister, Lady Naomi, never left the house without a trail of servants following her.

Stephen stopped petting Milton and leaned over to pick up a bottle of brandy from a side table. He held it up, but Harry shook his head. "Not at this hour. In fact, I think I might need to give the brandy and whisky a bit of a rest. I have a sneaking suspicion that I am going to have to get my hands dirty with this job," replied Harry.

The last thing he needed was to be deep in his cups when the occasion called for the use of his fists, or worse, a pistol. He might well be considered somewhat of a fop by much of the *ton*, but Harry had never let a client down yet. And he wasn't about to start.

"What else are you planning? A well-placed threat perhaps? I do find them quite effective," said Stephen.

I have a feeling this blackguard won't flinch if threatened. He has too much to lose if he backs off.

Harry sauntered over to the window. His head was now clear enough that he could risk looking out into the brightness of the mid-morning. On the street below, people moved up and down Grosvenor Street.

At least the weather is pleasant for seeing Mama at luncheon today.

His weekly catch-up with his mother in town was the highlight of his week. He might not be able to visit his family home but seeing her gave him hope for some reconciliation in the future.

"I'm not sure on the warning shot across his bow. I think a spot of reconnaissance is in order first. I want to get the measure of this Saint chap and to discover just how much of a hold he has over Miss Patience North. If she is but a passing fancy, a quiet word in his ear might well suffice."

Stephen poured himself a generous glass of brandy, then sat back. Harry didn't need to hear what his friend was likely thinking. Fortune hunters came in all forms, some downright dangerous. But they all shared the one attribute—dogged persistence. The minute they got a whiff of a pound note, the game was on.

"Let me know if you require a late-night roughing up of this blackguard. I am always available," replied Stephen.

"I am expecting an update from my spies at some point today, and then this evening, I shall head to Viscount Ashton's ball and get a good look at the situation for myself. I also want to have a longer conversation with Miss Alice North. There are a number of important questions for which I need answers from her."

"Such as?"

Harry turned from the window. "Well, for a start, there is the most obvious one, why the hell is an unmarried young woman having to ward off a possible family scandal? The second being, just how far is she prepared to go?"

Handing over her papa's hard-earned cash was one thing, but if they were going to get Cuthbert Saint out of the picture, Miss Alice North might have to step up to the mark.

She may have the spine for dealing with rude nobles, but

when push came to shove, would she have the stomach for standing beside him and confronting a desperate man?

Hmm. I have a feeling my Alice might just have that sort of fortitude.

He could only hope that things would not get so bad as to have to put his client in danger.

Chapter Three

"Oh, do come on, Alice. We will be late," moaned Patience.

Alice had dragged her heels for as long as she could, but there was no delaying the inevitable. Patience was determined to attend the ball and be seen on the arm of Cuthbert Saint.

Why couldn't you have fallen for a nice noble or at least a war hero? Anyone but him.

She could just imagine the look of abject horror on their mother's face if she was to witness her youngest daughter making a fool of herself over the charming Mister Saint. Mrs. North was all for her daughters living their own lives, but even she had her limits.

Pity those boundaries didn't stop you and Papa disappearing to Paris for three months.

"I'm coming," Alice replied.

After picking up her shawl, Alice draped it over her arm and hurried out of her bedroom. Downstairs, her sister paced back and forth. The moment Alice set foot on the ground floor, Patience took a firm hold of her arm and verily dragged her out the front door and into Mortimer Street.

"What is your hurry?" she pleaded.

An annoying grin appeared on Patience's face, and Alice immediately gritted her teeth. How many times had she seen that smile in the weeks since Cuthbert had sunk his claws into the youngest of the North siblings?

"Cuthbert said he is arriving early this evening. He wants to spend as much time as possible with me. He is even going to mark my dance card; can you believe it?" she said.

Oh yes, I can believe it. I expect he has plenty of plans to mark other parts of you as well, the dirty swine. Patience, how can you not see beyond his easy smile?

A footman assisted them both into the North family carriage. While Patience prattled on about the wonders of her handsome beau, Alice took the time to check that there were no stray pieces of lint on her dark grey gown. Flecks always showed up on the fabric.

Not exactly a green-and-yellow-floral gown. Nor is it accessorized with a piglet. I wonder what Lord Harry will make of it.

Not that she particularly cared what Harry Steele thought of her attire, but it was always nice to receive an approving glance from a gentleman. There were men within the *ton* who appreciated a well-made garment, and the modiste which her father's vast wealth afforded them was one of London's finest.

"Oh, I meant to tell you. A letter arrived from Ireland this morning," said Patience.

Alice stopped picking at her skirts and glared at her sister. The only person they knew in Ireland was their wastrel of a brother, Finn, who had bolted from the family home within days of their parents leaving for the continent.

"Why did you wait until now to tell me?" asked Alice.

Tears welled in Patience's eyes.

Oh, heaven help me. Don't become a watering pot when we are almost at the ball.

"I was going to tell you, but I knew you would get mad.

When you came home from wherever you had been this morning, you were in such a foul temper. I didn't want to add to your problems."

Alice took in a long, deep breath, trying her best to find her calm. "What did Finn's letter say?"

Patience dabbed at her face with her handkerchief but wouldn't meet Alice's eyes. If their brother intended to extend his impromptu journey to Ireland, she was going to kill him. So much for promising their parents that he would act as chaperone to his sisters during their absence.

"He said he was going to travel to Wexford to view some more horses."

Alice waited. There had to be more to Finn's note than that. Her brother was nothing if not predictable. He was also one hundred percent unreliable.

Is that a thing? Being reliably unreliable?

"What else did his letter say?" Alice leaned across the narrow carriage space and placed her hand on Patience's arm, giving it an encouraging rub. Her sister finally glanced her way.

"He has met someone. The daughter of a local landowner. Finn fancies himself in love and has vowed not to return to England until he has made her his wife."

Alice's hand slipped and it smacked against the leather of the carriage seat. With her head bowed, she let her fingers continue to tap while she tried to absorb this latest piece of unfortunate news.

With Finn remaining in Ireland, she was condemned to handle the growing disaster of her sister's foolish heart all on her own.

Why am I the only North sibling not under Cupid's spell?

The carriage finally turned into Green Street and pulled up out the front of Ashton House. With a heavy heart, Alice alighted and stood on the pavement. While she waited for Patience, she pondered a dark question.

Just how long would it take for her sister to forgive her if she happened to accidently put a bullet into Cuthbert Saint? Shooting him a second time might, however, be a little difficult to explain.

I am sorely tempted.

When she caught a glimpse of the happiness which radiated on Patience's face, Alice put all notions of villainy aside. That look told her all she needed to know. The only way that the North family was going to be rid of Mister Saint was by managing to unveil his true nature. For her to break her sister's heart.

As she followed a hurrying Patience up the front steps of Ashton House, Alice began to pray.

Please, dear lord, let Harry Steele be here tonight, and let him live up to his secret reputation. I don't know what I will do if he fails me.

Chapter Four

Lord and Lady Ashton's elegant mansion was the usual crush of people, but within seconds of their arrival, Cuthbert Saint had managed to locate the North sisters and was making his regular play. He bowed low to Alice, and she offered him a tight smile in reply.

When he turned his attention to Patience and gifted her with a heart-stopping smile, a tide of nausea rose in Alice's stomach. The man was so much like pond slime, she couldn't bear it.

Still, she had to give Cuthbert his dues. He was immaculately turned out, his jet-black hair perfectly oiled. The cut of his evening suit was so sharp, Alice was certain she would bleed if she touched it.

Why did you have to be so damn handsome? A flaw of any sort would be nice—just something I can highlight with Patience.

"Mister Saint, how wonderful to see you here this evening," gushed Patience.

"It is such an unexpected delight," he replied.

Even his voice is silken. Patience never stood a chance.

Cuthbert offered Patience his arm and led her away, leaving Alice standing alone and pondering further dire options. She was still considering whether it was worth the coin to hire a couple of thugs to pay him a visit when a loud cheer erupted close to the entrance to the main ballroom.

Alice turned as a large section of the crowd divided down the middle and a now familiar figure strode into the room. Men and women smiled and applauded alike at Lord Harry Steele. Fans and eyelashes were fluttered in his direction. Several women swooned.

Harry held out his arms and accepted their adulation. His gold walking stick was borne aloft like he was a biblical prophet.

"Gosh. Moses didn't get that good a reception when he parted the Red Sea, and he destroyed Pharaoh's army at the same time," she muttered.

To be fair, Alice didn't think Moses had ever worn a pure white suit. Nor a bright red codpiece. He most definitely hadn't sported a silver tiara. Harry's outfit was a riot of mismatched eccentricity.

And yet he wore it so well.

Other guests clamored for his attention. Hands were thrust out for shaking. Numerous glasses of champagne were quickly offered. Women dipped into low curtsies, the kind that allowed a man a good look at their breasts if he was so inclined.

Harry rewarded them all with a beaming smile. Talk about making an entrance.

And then his gaze met hers and Alice's heart stopped.

૨૦

Excellent. She was here. If Miss Alice North had not come to the Ashtons' ball tonight, all the hours Harry had dedicated to selecting an outfit and dressing for the party would have gone to waste.

She was wearing a shocked and thoroughly disapproving look. *Brilliant*. The outrageous outfit had worked.

What better way to have London thinking he was a brainless peacock than to dress and act like one in public? He was more than happy to let people believe that they were superior to him and his dandyish lifestyle. Those who were gushing all over him as he made his grand entrance were also the ones who would be making snide remarks about him behind his back, the second he was out of earshot.

And yet one by one, as scandals touched their lives, they would seek him out and pay for his assistance.

Harry wasn't the least fazed by their insincere behavior; he was counting on it. He was a master at being a chameleon. His father's library had contained many books, and the hours he had spent studying them meant he was well aware that the most dangerous creatures on earth were those who dazzled their victims just before they struck.

Waving the rest of his disingenuous fans away, Harry made a beeline for the corner where Miss Alice North lurked. He gave a deliberate sexy sway of his hips and her eyes immediately grew wide.

You are so easy to tease and tempt. If you weren't a client, I would love to . . . hmm.

He stopped a few feet away and bowed. "Miss North, what a pleasure," he all but purred.

Her gaze roamed slowly over his body. Harry opened his white jacket, showing off the gold lining, inviting her perusal. She might well be doing her utmost to look aghast at his attire, but he caught the telltale signs that she liked what she saw. The mere glint in her eyes. The hand she held softly to her chest. And the tongue that moistened her bottom lip. Oh. Yes.

"Lord Steele," she said.

Harry frowned. "No. Please. My friends call me Harry. We cannot be so formal with one another."

He had her money, and in his book, anyone who gave him cash was counted as a friend.

"Harry." She accepted his offered arm and he led her out of the corner and to a private alcove away from the crush of guests. Even as she took a seat on a cream sofa, her gaze remained fixed on his outfit.

I knew the tiara was the right choice.

His sparkling costume was a stark contrast to her attire. He didn't even want to consider the dull, dark grey of Alice's gown. He could see what she had been trying to achieve—the blank-canvas look—but all it did was make him feel sorry for her.

Is pity a color?

Resisting the temptation to sit close to her, Harry took up a seat at the end of the sofa and kept a respectable distance between them. Alice was wringing her hands in an obvious display of discomfort. "I . . . I'm not sure if you are the man for the job," she said.

He let out a long, seductive sigh. In every contract, there came a time when his clients panicked. When they truly believed that the sum of all he was amounted to what they beheld with their eyes. This moment was always heavily pregnant with risk.

He leaned in and whispered in her ear, "But if I do that, your sweet sister will end up marrying that scoundrel. You owe it to her and your family to use all means necessary to stop that happening. And that includes trusting me."

The seriousness of his tone seemed to have the desired effect. Alice screwed her eyes shut and clenched her lips between her teeth. Harry always hated this part. When he had to break his clients down in order to help rebuild them and gain their trust.

"You think me a fool, but I promise I will save Patience. From my initial investigations, your instincts about Cuthbert

Saint appear to be sound. But before I go into that, I need to ask you some questions," he said.

She frowned at him. "What sort of questions?"

"Well for a start, where the devil are your parents? They can't be blind as to what is happening. But probably of even greater importance is the question of how far you are prepared to go in order to help your sister."

If it came to it, would Alice be prepared to hold a pistol and point it at Cuthbert Saint?

Chapter Five

❦

Alice could just imagine how this all looked to Harry. She came from new money. Established London society tended to hold an unfavorable opinion of her people. It was said that people who had made their money in trade had nice houses and good clothes, but no common sense or breeding.

Her folk didn't lack breeding; they had been landed gentry sometime in the dim and distant past. The North family had fallen on hard times only to resurrect their fortunes through trade with the colonies. Her father could buy most of the assembled guests here several times over and have change in his pocket.

And they would still look down on him.

Unfortunately, the gibe about a lack of common sense was a little more accurate. Her parents had raised their children in a free-living household. They had been allowed to choose their own bedtimes from an early age. Few restrictions had been placed on any of the North siblings as they grew up. And at times, it showed.

But even her parents would draw the line at Patience marrying a fortune hunter.

"You mean why haven't Mama and Papa put a stop to all

this nonsense? They are somewhere in France. They are not expected back in England until Christmas at the earliest. I cannot wait to do something until they return, because I fear by then it will all be too late," she replied.

She could just imagine what Harry was thinking right this very minute. What kind of parents trotted off to Europe and left their unwed daughters behind? The reckless kind.

But she wasn't paying him to pass judgement on her family. Harry had a task, and if he wasn't up to it, then he had better say so.

He slowly shook his head. "And I thought my family were a disaster. My mother subscribed to the same sort of madness for a time. She got mixed up with the Cavendish crowd who tended to let their offspring run wild. Fortunately, my father finally saw sense and put his foot down."

"I wouldn't say my parents have raised us in complete chaos. They have just allowed us to make our own mistakes and learn from them."

I can't believe I am having to defend my family to a man wearing a red codpiece and a tiara.

Harry brushed a hand over Alice's cheek. She held her breath. He was the strangest creature she had ever met, but there was something about him which drew her in. If handsome men like Cuthbert Saint were Patience's weakness, perhaps interesting and slightly oddball chaps like Harry Steele were hers.

He wagged a ring-laden finger in her direction, disapproval evident in his voice. "But you are not prepared to let your sister make her own mistake when it comes to Mister Saint. So, what you are saying is that your free spirit only goes so far. Considering your own propensity to wander the streets of London on your own, some may suggest that your attitude could be construed as more than a little hypocritical."

She shot him a hard glare. "Others may say that of me, but I don't care. You know as well as I do that marriage is a mistake which cannot be easily erased if one does not choose their life partner wisely," she bit back.

A shrewd smile crept to his lips. Damn him. He was testing her. Alice wanted nothing more than to grab a hold of Harry's beautifully constructed suit and crush it in her hands. And then bludgeon him with his walking stick. *Condescending, self-assured rogue.*

"Good. Then you have the right mindset for what needs to be done," he replied.

She blinked at him. He was agreeing with her. She hadn't seen that coming. "What sort of mindset?"

"One that is capable of making hard decisions. We need to rid your sister of Cuthbert Saint, or whatever his real name is, because I would have a guinea on him not being any sort of saint."

It was a struggle to keep up with Harry. One minute, he was all light and ridiculousness. The next, he was planning a war strategy.

"What do you know about him?" she asked.

"A little. I have my contacts checking the rest of his supposed life story. According to my sources, he claims to have attended Eton and also worked somewhere in a government ministry. It shouldn't be too big a task to get to the truth of his history, after which we can pull on the loose threads and see which ones begin to unravel."

He waved over a passing footman and collected them both a glass of champagne. Alice stared at hers, unsure as to whether it was wise to drink it. Patience and Cuthbert had already disappeared from the ballroom and she should make an effort to track them down.

Her gaze searched the immediate area, but they were too far out of the way for her to get any real idea as to who was in the room. She went to rise.

"I must go and find them. Lord knows where they are."

He took her gently by the arm and pulled her back onto

the sofa. "Drink your champagne and try to relax. I have several people watching them. The minute Cuthbert makes a move to whisk your sister into a dark corner of the garden, he will find himself in the company of new and rather insistent friends."

"How did you manage that?"

"I made a grand entrance just now, but I actually arrived some time ago, and while swathed in a black hooded cloak and staying out of sight, I observed Mister Saint."

She bit back tears and whispered, "Thank you." Finally, someone was on her side. The spark of hope which lit her heart almost made Alice giddy.

At times, it was like she was alone in being the only sensible one in her family—never more so than in the current circumstances. Her parents were several hundred miles away, her brother somewhere loose in Ireland, and as for her sister . . .

Alice was beginning to get a sense of Harry. The man behind the showy exterior. One who, it would seem, was in possession of a sharp mind. It was comforting to know that she had underestimated him.

Perhaps you are the man for the job.

He sipped at his champagne. From the way he barely drank any of it, Alice could tell he didn't particularly like the bubbles.

When their gazes met, he raised an eyebrow. "If I drink sensible, manly spirits like brandy or whisky in public, it makes me appear too much like other men. I expect you have already perceived that my intent is to stand apart from them. For people to find me a source of interest and amusement."

She nodded. "Yes, I had gathered that. I also think you do it deliberately as a sleight-of-hand. People think one thing of you while you are doing something else entirely. It is a clever trick."

The wicked grin he gave in response to her words had

Alice swallowing deeply. She was drawn to this dangerous man—wanted to know so much more about him. He was the most interesting man in the room.

He set his champagne glass on the floor and she followed suit.

"Can I ask you a question?" she ventured. Harry was the son of one of the richest men in all of England; he shouldn't have to work. Everyone knew the Duke of Redditch got about town in a gilded coach.

"Hmm. And the answer is I need the money."

How had he known what she was going to ask? *Am I that easy to read?*

"I did some things which did not sit well with my father. I am a fourth son. We are usually relegated to the church, or the army, or some far-flung foreign post. I refused to do any of that, and he didn't take too kindly to my impertinence," he explained.

"So, he cut you off?" Alice had heard of such things, but until now had never actually met a disinherited son. She had thought they were simply rumors put about by parents to make their offspring behave. But in Harry she was getting her first real glimpse of what refusing to toe the line could mean to the son of a noble house.

"Yes. Not a penny. Threw me out of the house almost a year ago and told me not to come back. Two days out from Christmas Eve, if you don't mind. Fortunately, I have friends, and we'd already been working on a plan to make money. We each use our particular skills to earn a living. In my case, that is scandals. I used to start them; now I manage them."

Hearing his words, Alice's heart grew light. Harry Steele might well be the most bizarre and uncommon man she had ever met, but there was something about him that gave her the courage to continue. Strengthened her resolve to save Patience from making a grave error. "Harry, if you can rid Patience of her blind devotion to Cuthbert Saint, I will double your fee," she said. She held out her hand, intending it to be for them to seal the deal.

Harry took one look at it, grabbed a hold, and pulled Alice to him. Before she could object, he had placed a soft, tender kiss on her lips.

Harry's arm went around her waist and he held her captive in his embrace. As his tongue slipped into her mouth, Alice thought to slap his arm. His behavior was outrageous, beyond the pale. She was his client. They were in Viscount Ashton's home. The whole thing was simply impossible.

And yet, she was powerless to stop him.

All her sense of control and decorum went straight out the window as Harry deepened the kiss. What he was doing with his soft, warm lips set her heart racing at a furious pace. If she fainted away in a deep swoon it wouldn't surprise her in the least.

And I wouldn't care, just as long as it was in his arms.

Alice could have sworn her heart let out a pained whimper when Harry finally released her from the kiss and loosened his hold. She held a hand to her pounding chest, sucking in deep breaths. What on earth had just happened?

When their gazes met once more, a pair of cool green eyes stared back at her. There was a mischievous light in them—one Alice didn't trust.

As a sly, knowing grin crept across Harry's face. The happy bubbles which had danced delightfully in Alice's stomach only a moment ago burst. Pop. Pop. Pop.

In their place sat a burning, simmering anger.

"See, I knew you were the sort of girl who a man could kiss in public and she wouldn't stop him." He leaned in close and whispered in her ear, "Alice, darling, I understand you better than you think. You can try and deny it all you like, but deep inside you know given half a chance, you would hand your soul over to a man like Cuthbert Saint. Or even a man like me."

Alice's hand landed at high speed on Harry's face. The bright mark which immediately colored his left cheek was deeply satisfying.

Bloody, self-assured, arrogant . . . urgh!

"I take back my words of praise. You, Lord Harry Steele, are nothing better than a scoundrel."

He lifted a hand to his reddened skin, then slowly shook his head. "Not a scoundrel—just a rogue." His eyes glinted with danger. "And the only man with the skills and daring to save your sister."

Chapter Six

Harry made his way over to the offices of the RR Coaching Company in Gracechurch Street the following morning. The small coaching business which operated as the cover for the group's illicit operations was situated next door to the Spread Eagle Coaching Company.

But while their neighbors ran a highly respectable establishment, managing coach routes all over England, the small office door marked RR fronted a more secretive and less reputable place. It was the perfect setting for the Rogues of the Road to conduct their dubious business transactions.

The old coach which had been abandoned in the rear yard was now repaired and being used to transport smuggled goods up from Portsmouth. If things all went well and they had enough money, Harry and Monsale intended to launch a legitimate passenger service in the near future.

However, on this overcast morning, Harry's thoughts were not of coach timetables but rather Cuthbert Saint. Who was he, and where had he come from? Only once he had a firm understanding of the man would Harry be able to put together a plan to unmask Patience North's paramour and bring the blighter down.

After tethering his horse in the rear mews, Harry scraped the thick Thames River mud from his boots. He had ridden most of the way over on the main roads, but walked the last half mile along the riverbank, turning north just near London Bridge. As per standard procedure, he checked over his shoulder as he stepped away from the river and headed toward Gracechurch Street. Anyone foolish enough to be following him would be easily spotted.

Making his way over to the wooden steps which led to the top floor of the sixteenth-century stone building, he touched his fingers to his cheek. Alice North had a fearsome temper on her. He was sure he could still feel the sting from when her palm had landed on his face.

"Ah yes, you had to get a blow in for propriety's sake, Alice, but we both know you enjoyed it," he muttered.

She had kissed him back, even relaxed into the embrace. Her response to his ungentlemanly behavior had been exactly what he had hoped for; she had a passionate heart. She was stubborn as a mule, but that was part of her charm. Easy wins were not worth having.

And yet you still chased after her when she left the alcove and headed back into the main ballroom. You couldn't let her go without getting a final word in.

He paused as his foot settled on the bottom step. That kiss had simply been to confirm his suspicions about Alice, but he couldn't stop thinking about it.

Lord knew he had kissed plenty of women in the past. Harry was the master of loving and leaving, and not always caring about breaking the occasional heart.

As he climbed the stairs, a cold sense of dread began to fill his mind. Alice had affected him in a way he couldn't decipher. She was different, and it scared him more than just a little.

While her assessment of him being a scoundrel was close to the mark, he wasn't completely devoid of emotions. He had just perfected the art of keeping them well under control.

Or I thought I had.

At the height of their kiss, he had sensed his power slipping, shifting. The moment she had offered up her tongue and touched his, it was Alice who had taken command. And he had let her.

What is wrong with me? I need to go home and have a tonic as soon as I am finished here. I must be coming down with something.

He pushed the thought of her deep hazel eyes to the back of his mind. He didn't need a hand mirror to know that a worried look sat on his face, and he most certainly didn't need his friends asking what was troubling him.

If I told them it was a woman, they would laugh themselves sick.

Reaching the top of the steps, he stopped and considered the heavy oak door. On the other side of it was the one place in all of London he felt welcome and safe. He took a deep calming breath and reached for the door handle.

"Get a hold of yourself, man. You are a rogue. Act like one."

Harry pulled hard on the door, and with a tight smile on his lips, made his way inside.

The moment he set foot in the room, he was greeted with the familiar smell of cigars and burning wood. He was home.

Two other members of the RR Coaching Company were seated around the long walnut dining table. Almost every inch of its surface was covered in knife marks, but at least it was now kept clean. Stephen was lounging on a nearby Chesterfield sofa.

"Morning all," Harry said.

Stephen gave him a chin tip. Monsale and George each lifted a finger. The only member of the Rogues of the Road absent this morning was Gus. He and the coach were currently somewhere between London and Portsmouth, bringing in another illegal shipment from France.

Monsale stepped away from the table and came to greet his fellow rogue. They shook hands, after which Harry handed over a small bag of coins. "My contribution to the rent. I should have more money by the end of the week."

Monsale tucked the bag into his coat pocket. "How did the ball go last night? Did you make much headway with the North sisters?"

Harry shrugged. It was rare for him to reveal much of his current projects, but for the notional leader of the band of miscreants, he would make an exception. He had asked Monsale to help with some of the preliminary investigations.

"I got a good look at Cuthbert Saint; he strikes me as a rotten little shit who needs some violence brought upon his person. And of course, Patience North is utterly besotted with him," he replied.

Monsale turned up his nose. "What about the other sister? The one who engaged your services? Could you make use of her?"

Now there is a double entendre just waiting to be spoken.

Harry had thoroughly kissed Alice last night, but he was still a gentleman. He may well be thinking of what he would like to use her for, but he wouldn't dare give it voice. "She has a sensible head on her shoulders and is determined to separate the two young lovers. It turns out the North parents are some free-spirited new money romantics who think nothing of leaving their unwed daughters in England while they trip off to Europe for a grand tour."

George tutted his disgust. His father was a member of the judiciary, and as a result, George was probably the most traditional thinker of the group. If anyone wanted to know how society would view their misdeeds if they ever came to light, they could rely upon him. What his magistrate father would say if he were ever to discover his son's career as a professional thief was, of course, another matter.

"What is your plan?" asked George.

Harry had been mulling a few details in his mind during the journey over from Grosvenor Street. Picking holes in Cuthbert's history seemed the obvious one.

"I'm going to press Miss Alice into service, and through her, get close to our Mister Saint. A few difficult questions dropped in at the pertinent time should give him something to worry about. From the way the younger North sister was staring all doe-eyed at him last night, I think the sooner I move the better."

Stephen rose from the sofa and gave a yawn. "Which means, you will be thinking to pay a visit to Cuthbert Saint's current place of residence. I have managed to locate him at the Grand Hotel in Covent Garden."

Harry let out a low whistle. The Grand Hotel was one of London's premier establishments. A man would need coin to be able to stay in such a fine place.

"That's interesting. If he can afford the Grand, one has to ponder the question of how he is funding himself right now. I will do some more digging and see what I can find. Meanwhile, I sent word this morning to Miss Alice, asking her to bring her sister to a charity do this evening," he replied.

"I thought you avoided charity events like the plague," said Stephen.

"Yes, well, I'm not exactly flush with funds," replied Harry.

Monsale sighed and put his hand into his coat pocket, retrieving the coin purse. He handed it back to Harry. "For heaven's sake, man, make sure you hand that over when you get in the front door. It doesn't look good for one's image if you appear to be miserly with your money."

The Duke of Monsale was always far more concerned with keeping up the appearance of wealth than the rest of the group, something which Harry often put to good use. He took the money. "Alright. I shall make certain that people see me parting with coins. But I still consider this month's rent paid."

After a quick drink, he hurried back downstairs, eager to follow up on Stephen's lead and visit the Grand Hotel.

Tossing the bag of coins in the air, he chuckled. "Two birds, one stone."

He had money for the charity donation; now he just had to get Miss Alice North to agree with his plans and hand over more of her lovely coin.

I wonder if she might throw another kiss in with the bargain?

Harry headed for the stables and his horse. Thoughts of Alice and the delight of spending yet another evening in her company would have to wait. Right now, he had another matter to concern himself with—Mister Cuthbert Saint and his lavish lifestyle. Why would a man with apparent means be haunting Patience North's footsteps?

He snorted at the obvious answer. "Because one can never have too much money."

Chapter Seven

The Grand Hotel, Covent Garden, was a favorite of the *ton*, and certainly lived up to its name. It offered the sort of lavish suites that few other hotels in London did. Many well-to-do families stayed there when visiting town.

Even the rear mews, where coaches and horses were stabled, were of a higher standard than what was normally found in the usual run-of-the-mill coaching and travel inns. It cost Harry the princely sum of a shilling to tip the stable boy. He was still grumbling about the coin as he made his way inside.

Then he caught sight of the hotel foyer and his eyes lit up.

Oh, this is rather nice. Reminds me of home.

His gaze took in the deep green-and-gold-striped carpets, as well as the matching drapes. From the style of the elegant silver chandeliers which lit the foyer, Harry was certain the hotel had engaged the same overpriced decorator his mother had used to refurbish her grand drawing room at Redditch House.

The place oozed money. It was exactly where a man hoping to create a façade of wealth would choose to stay.

A footman hurried over and greeted him. "Good morning, sir. May I have your luggage brought in from your coach?"

"Thank you, no. I am here to visit a friend who is staying at the hotel. A Mister Saint," he replied.

"Ah, of course. Should I have a note sent up to him to let him know you have arrived?"

"Well, actually, this visit was a bit of a spur-of-the-moment thing. So, my friend isn't expecting me. If you let me know which room he is in, I could just nip upstairs and give him a big surprise." Harry dug into his coat pocket and withdrew a shilling. He handed it to the footman who, after taking one look at it, promptly cleared his throat. Harry sighed, and with great reluctance, reached into his pocket and retrieved a second coin.

Two shillings. I could buy a pair of stockings for that!

"Mister Saint is in room one hundred and twelve. If you take the stairs and turn right at the top, you will find his room located along the hall," replied the footman, slipping the coins into his waistcoat.

Harry and his ever-decreasing purse quickly headed upstairs. He found Cuthbert Saint's room soon enough—but kept walking as he passed.

The door suddenly opened, and he barely had time to scoot into a nearby alcove before Cuthbert stepped out. He closed the door behind him and locked it. Harry risked a peek from his hiding spot and caught a glimpse of Cuthbert's back as he made his way to the stairs.

Talk about perfect timing.

He now had the golden opportunity to do a little light snooping around Cuthbert's room. He was fishing around in his pocket for his set of skeleton keys when Cuthbert made an unexpected reappearance, trailed by the footman. Harry darted out of sight, praying he had not been seen.

"I assure you, Mister Saint, I sent your friend up here not

five minutes ago. Are you certain you didn't pass him on the stairs?"

Bloody hell. I forgot about him. Talk about being too damned efficient at your job.

"No. I saw no one. Could you describe the man for me?" replied Cuthbert.

Harry's morning was quickly descending into farce. So much for his plans for a simple spot of breaking and entering.

"Average height. Dark hair. Well-dressed," said the footman.

Harry gave a small sigh of relief. The footman's description could very well match any other guest in the hotel, as well as half of London.

"Well, he is not here. Perhaps he headed back downstairs," replied Cuthbert.

After waiting until the sound of footsteps had disappeared, Harry then stepped out from the alcove. He dared not risk taking the main stairs, nor trying to break into the room. Getting out of the hotel unseen was now his main concern. Taking the skeleton key from his pocket, he headed for the door at the end of the hall. It wouldn't be the first nor the last time he would leave an establishment by way of the servants' entrance.

It was only as he was exiting the hotel grounds that Harry's luck finally took a turn for the better. He caught sight of Cuthbert Saint climbing into a hack on the other side of Bow Street.

In a flash, he was across the road and hailing the next carriage. "Follow that one in front and don't lose him," he said.

What had started out as a sly piece of reconnaissance had morphed into an unexpected chase.

The hack slowed and moved to the side of the street. Harry pressed his face to the glass and smiled as his second piece of fortune came into view.

Jones and Son. He had never been happier to see the sign with three gold balls hanging over the doorway of one of London's foremost pawnbrokers. An establishment which Cuthbert Saint had just walked into.

This is a spot of brilliant luck.

After handing over yet more coins, Harry alighted from the carriage and went into the small coffee house next door. He had plenty of time for a hot drink and a sticky bun. There was no need for him to risk being seen. Unbeknownst to him, Cuthbert Saint was doing business with one of the RR Coaching Company's connections.

By the time Harry did eventually leave Jones and Son, he had all the information he needed to confirm his suspicions that Cuthbert was handling stolen goods and pawning them as he went. From the small inexpensive item, he had sold this morning, it was clear that Patience North's beau was fast running out of money.

Harry headed back to Grosvenor Street and penned a note to Alice, instructing her as to what she was to do next.

The time had come to tighten the screws on Cuthbert Saint.

Chapter Eight

He'd kissed her and now he was making demands.
I cannot believe the nerve of this man.

Lord Harry Steele was a man in possession of the world's biggest sense of self-worth. Yet, even as she read his note for the third time, there was no doubt in Alice's mind that she was going to do exactly what he asked of her.

Yes, he was rude. Yes, he was pompous. And while she hated to admit it to herself, he was the one man in all of London right now whom she was prepared to trust with her sister's future.

The man is a scoundrel as well as a rogue. I just wish he didn't make me so confused.

In the short time since she had known him, Alice had experienced a number of emotions and sensations that were far outside of her previous experience. And that had been before Harry had kissed her.

What a pity he is such a damn good kisser.

For heaven's sake, stop thinking about it. It wasn't that great a kiss.

Oh, alright, yes it was. He kissed me senseless and made my toes curl.

Blinking, Alice's focus settled once more on Patience, seated across the carriage from her. Patience was still talking. She was certain her sister hadn't stopped since they'd left Lord Ashton's ball the previous night.

I wish this carriage would hurry up. Why does it take so long to journey anywhere in London?

Slipping the note from Harry into her reticule, she went back to listening to Patience as she continued to prattle on about the wonder that was Mister Cuthbert Saint.

Patience leaned across the carriage and smiled at her. She put a hand into the top of her bodice and a gold necklace suddenly appeared between her fingers. It had a small heart-shaped locket hanging on the end of it. Alice had never seen the piece of jewelry before.

Her blood ran cold at the sight of it.

"Cuthbert gave it to me last night at the ball. Isn't it divine? He says he hopes to be giving me more tokens of his affection very soon," she said.

Sweet lord, that could mean anything. What if he gets her pregnant?

Alice could only pray that Harry had good news to impart when she saw him shortly. Anything that would see the back of Cuthbert would be a godsend.

"Cuthbert says we shall supper together this evening. And Cuthbert promised me a dance. Did I mention that Cuthbert will be in attendance at the ball? Isn't that marvelous?" cooed Patience.

Alice did her best to ignore the twitch in the corner of her eye. She dared not put her thoughts of Cuthbert into words, lest she say something that might cause serious offence. Staring out the carriage window was a more prudent idea. Besides, the dark streets of London held greater appeal than listening to Patience drone on about Cuthbert Saint.

The ride from Mortimer Street to the Royal Chelsea Hospital, where the charity gala was taking place, took an inordinate amount of time. The distance itself was only three miles, but central London at this time of night was packed with carriages heading in all manner of directions.

As she continued to watch the passing traffic, Alice's mind wandered back yet again to Harry and *that* kiss. She lifted a gloved hand to her lips. It had been almost twenty-four hours since he'd pressed his warm mouth to hers, but she could have sworn she could still feel the heat of his touch.

Alice North wasn't a complete innocent. She had been kissed before, but those experiences had been nothing like what Lord Harry Steele had done. He had rocked her to the bottom of her heavily beaded evening slippers.

The man needs to be locked up, kept away from women. Or at least other women.

Pity the poor girl who did end up marrying him. She would spend every social function fighting off the attentions of Harry's legion of female fans.

"Who was the gentleman I saw you with last night?" asked Patience.

Alice vaguely stirred from her musings. "What?"

Patience huffed. "You were talking to an oddly dressed gentleman last night and I was asking who he was."

Blast. She hadn't realized Patience had witnessed her and Harry talking. She had to think quick.

But she cannot have seen too much.

"Which gentleman?" Alice replied, playing dumb.

"Which gentleman? Why, the one in the white suit with the foolish tiara on his head. Who else? Everyone was staring at him. I saw you and he exchange some brief words when Cuthbert and I returned to the main ballroom," said Patience.

Alice let a slow breath out. Her sister had seen a mere snippet of her encounter with Harry. Seen him after he had followed her out of the alcove.

"Oh . . . him. That was Lord Harry Steele. He was

attempting to get me to comment on his codpiece. I told him he was a silly man and to leave me alone," she replied.

"I see."

For the first time in her life, Alice was grateful when Patience went back to singing the praises of Cuthbert Saint. Anything to take her sister's attention away from her and Harry.

At the Royal Chelsea Hospital, a now familiar pattern repeated itself. No sooner had they set foot inside, and while Alice was still handing over a banker's instruction payable to the hospital, than Cuthbert appeared.

Alice was immediately abandoned by her lovestruck sister, who hurried away.

"Really, Patience! Not even a goodbye?" she huffed.

"Steady your hand."

She turned at the voice and was greeted with the surprising sight of Harry in almost regulation evening attire. The half dozen strands of pearls around his neck were the only concession to his usual madcap method of dressing.

"What do you mean?" she replied.

"Let's talk somewhere a little more private," said Harry.

He guided her away from the donation desk and waited until they were out of earshot of anyone before he spoke again. "I mean, keep your nerve steady. Men like Mister Saint thrive on chaos. If you start to lose your temper in front of him and your beloved sister, he will have her siding with him in no time. And I can assure you that is the last thing we want. She has to be able to see him with her own eyes. She won't be able to do that if she is looking through the lens of pity."

Alice nodded toward an area to one side of the Great Hall designed by Sir Christopher Wren himself. She couldn't risk Patience seeing the two of them together.

He followed her over, a scowl sitting firmly knitted on his

brow. Harry was clearly not a man used to being given instructions. "What is the problem?" he asked.

"You and I are the problem. And I don't just mean *that* kiss," she replied. "Patience saw us talking last night. She mentioned it in the carriage ride over here. I had to make up some cock-and-bull story about your codpiece to throw her off the scent."

The furrow in his brow smoothed out a little. "Good. It means you are prepared to think on your feet. But not to worry. We made great progress today, and I intend to capitalize on it tonight."

"Meaning?"

"Cuthbert Saint is a fortune hunter. He is currently living off the money he gets from pawning small items of value. Trinkets which I expect he has stolen from others. My connections tell me that he is down to the last two or three decent pieces."

Alice held her reticule tightly in her hand, quietly strangling it. How could this be good news?

"He will be getting desperate to secure Patience's hand in marriage, and with that will come missteps. Trust me. He will make a mistake. We just need to make sure that your sister sees it when it happens."

When Harry took a hold of her trembling hand, Alice didn't stop him. His firm grip was the solid reassurance she so desperately craved. They were in this together.

"I want you to go and find Patience and Cuthbert. Engage in polite, dare I say, friendly conversation with him. I will come over at some point and introduce myself. You need to play along with my plan. I am going to see if we can trip our friend up."

"Alright. Give me a minute to summon my courage. You might be well-acquainted with matters of deception, but I am not," she replied.

He lifted her gloved hand to his lips and placed a kiss on

each finger. She shivered at his touch. *Oh.* How could such a small thing make her feel so good?

Harry...

If he attempted to kiss her a second time, she wasn't entirely sure what she would do. When it came to Harry, Alice no longer trusted herself.

"I think you are capable of much more than you give yourself credit for, sweet Alice. And I intend to show you just how great you could be, even if it means having my face slapped on a regular basis," he said.

Alice's heart thumped hard in her chest as Harry released her hand and slipped away into the crowd. She was pinning her hopes on his words merely being a tool to get her to do his bidding.

But what if they weren't? What if he was truly the first person who could actually see the woman she tried to keep hidden from the world? If he could understand her very nature?

Well then, I haven't the faintest idea what I will do.

§⋅

Harry's gaze constantly tracked across the room, missing little. The gathering was much like most other events attended by London's social elite. He caught the occasional glimpse of a shared smile between secret lovers. The glare of enemies who were forced to behave as friends in public. And the heartbreaking look of longing on a young man's face as he watched the woman, he loved walk across the room arm in arm with her new husband.

That last one had been a particular success of his, but it had been bittersweet—especially for the bride and the beau she would have married, had said beau been in possession of a title. Her parents had been determined to see their daughter become a baroness. Fortunes and reputations had been saved from a shocking scandal, but hearts had paid a high price. Even Harry had been left bruised and reflective of whether it had all been worth it.

Concentrate. That job is done and dusted. There is nothing anyone can do but hope that time heals.

It was time to put his Lord-Harry-Steele-foppish-fool act into play. After grabbing two glasses of champagne, he made his way over to where Alice, Patience, and his prey stood. Alice caught his eye for the briefest of moments, then turned away.

Good girl. Play it nice and easy. Steady nerves.

He crashed into the side of Cuthbert Saint, spilling most of a full glass of champagne down the side of Cuthbert's evening jacket.

"Oh! I am so bloody sorry!" While the liquid soaked into the fabric, Harry flailed his arms about and continued to offer up his apologies. "I am such a clumsy creature. Anyone would think I can't handle my drink. Here, take these."

He held the two glasses out to Alice, slopping more liquid onto the carpet. She took them and quickly handed them to a passing footman.

Harry took his cue from her move. "I didn't mean for you to get rid of them! I planned to drink what was left. But not to worry. There is plenty of free-flowing champagne here tonight. Did you make a donation at the door?"

His gaze had settled firmly on Cuthbert Saint. If he was going to unmask him as a moneygrubbing blackguard, he may as well start with the man's lack of charity.

"I posted a bank note," replied Cuthbert. The line sounded well-rehearsed.

I bet you haven't parted with a penny.

Harry thrust out his hand, and a drenched Cuthbert reluctantly took it.

"Lord Harry Steele. Papa is the Duke of Redditch," he said.

Cuthbert's cool demeanor warmed at the mention of one of the wealthiest men in England. He bowed his head. "Cuthbert Saint at your service, Lord Steele."

Harry pointed to the champagne mess on Cuthbert's jacket. "Terribly sorry about that. Not sure how you will get the stains out."

"Blotting it with a clean cloth and then letting it dry should do the trick," replied Cuthbert.

Harry's quick mind registered that tidy piece of information, storing it away for later perusal. He was certain he could ask a hundred other gentlemen in the place this evening if they knew how to treat champagne stains and he wouldn't get that sort of answer. A man with money had valets and servants to deal with those sorts of minor matters. But a man without funds might have to do it himself.

Cuthbert held out his hand and gestured toward Alice and Patience. "Your lordship, may I present Miss Alice and Miss Patience North."

Cuthbert had obviously done his homework and learned how London society worked when it came to be making correct introductions.

Harry bowed low. "Ladies, it is a pleasure to make your acquaintance. Though Miss Alice and I had words at Lord Ashton's ball last night, did we not?"

When Alice slowly looked him up and down, Harry could have dragged her into his arms and kissed her senseless. She was showing him the perfect amount of disinterest.

"Yes, Lord Steele. You seemed to think that it was acceptable to wear a codpiece to a formal function, whereas I disagreed. It is apparent that you also don't understand how to behave when you spill champagne on a gentleman's evening attire. A simple apology does not suffice."

"Yes, of course, where are my manners? Mister Saint, if you send your jacket to my house, I shall have my valet attend to it forthwith. It should only take a day or so for the wool to dry and then you may have it back. Better still, give it to me tonight and I shall take it with me," said Harry.

Cuthbert blanched at the offer, and Harry's expectations rose. A gentleman of society would likely have a number of evening jackets, but a scam artist looking to make an heiress his bride probably only had the one.

"It is fine. The jacket is not a problem. I shall have my valet deal with it," replied Cuthbert.

Recalling that Cuthbert had claimed to have attended Eton College, Harry moved in for the kill. "You don't trust to have your clothes laundered by others. I can't blame you. I remember the mess the servants at Eton used to make with our cricket caps. The stripes always came back dirtier than when we came off the field."

Cuthbert smiled and nodded. "Yes, I sent mine back several times when I was playing at Eton. I mean, how hard is it to get stripes clean?"

Patience shifted on her feet, and Harry took that as his signal to leave. He had enough to go on with for the evening. "Forgive me, I have intruded on your private gathering. And once again, I must apologize for my clumsiness."

He gave a hasty bow and left.

Outside in the street, his carriage and George Hawkins were waiting. The master thief was leaning against the side of the coach, smoking a small cheroot cigar, looking for all the world like he didn't have a care. Harry knew better. George would have been watching every person who entered the Great Hall of Royal Chelsea Hospital and be keeping a private tally of the worth of their jewels.

As Harry approached, George dropped the cheroot on the ground and stubbed it out. "How did it go? Do you have what you need?"

Harry nodded. "Not only is the blackguard a fortune hunter, he is a hopeless liar. He owns only the one evening jacket, and the blighter never went to Eton. I would say that was more than enough to make a move on him, but we need to be sure."

If Cuthbert Saint had attended Eton College, he would know full well that the school cricket cap was a solid light blue.

But bitter experience had taught Harry to measure twice and only then be ready to cut. He was all for checking things a third time.

"You want to know where he comes from and how he came by those pieces of jewelry?" asked George.

If Harry was going to confront Cuthbert, he had to have something to hold over him. A small white lie about his schooling and a penchant for living beyond his means was not enough. "I need Stephen and Monsale to continue following up rumors. People don't tend to move too far from the truth when they lie, which has me thinking that Cuthbert Saint was once in service. If we start looking for someone who might have worked in a great house and then suddenly went missing, we might secure a lead as to this scoundrel's true identity."

Until he had more information, there was not a lot he could do. He had eyes on all the coaching companies, and Gretna Green was covered. He would have to trust his friends to do some fast and deep digging.

While he waited, he would keep a close watch on things and make certain that Patience didn't come to harm. Biding his time would also allow him the opportunity to be with his client.

"And what about the other sister?" said George.

Their gazes met. A sly, knowing grin sat on the lips of the Honorable George Hawkins. There was a price to pay for spending one's life in the company of liars and thieves. They could read people as well as Harry did.

"I'm not sure. You know mixing business with pleasure is something I try to avoid, but she has me intrigued. Something tells me that behind her façade of sense and reason lies a woman of such passionate and captivating nature that a man could never tire of being with her," he replied.

George let out a low whistle. "Those are the words of a man who is clearly in Cupid's sights. You poor deluded bastard. It pains me to think you may already be beyond our aid."

Harry reached for the door of his carriage. "Are you coming?"

"Not a chance. I hear that such kinds of affection are contagious, and the last thing I wish is to fall for the charms of some sweet-faced chit. Besides, there is a tempting piece of Crusader treasure rumored to be arriving on the tide from Brest late tonight. I might just have to help it ashore."

If only Harry's life was that simple. Handling stolen goods was always risky, but jewels didn't have their own opinions. Nor did they have the same effect on a man that a woman such as Alice North did.

Rubies and sapphires could shine bright all they wished, but only a woman could make Harry Steele's blood run hot and his manhood rock hard.

The sooner he could kiss Alice once more, the better. Only then might he discover if what he felt for her was just a passing fancy or if it was something which went much deeper.

Chapter Nine

❧

Alice softly smiled. She had already caught the movement out of the corner of her eye but didn't wish to make it obvious that she had seen him. He was playing a game, darting in and out of the bookshelves, and despite her better judgement, she found herself eagerly wishing to play along.

While others may have viewed it as a childish indulgence of hide-and-go-seek, her racing heart told her otherwise. This was a prelude to something delicious and wicked.

She hurried down the long row of shelves, stopping at the end and standing with her back against the wood. Of course, if he wanted to find her, he only had to look for the check pattern of her skirts which hung out either side of the bookcases.

She waited, listening for footfalls on the carpet. Nothing. In the distance, another customer asked a shop assistant for a copy of *Emma* by Jane Austen.

Read it. In fact, I have read all her books. She is fabulous.

Alice even knew which shelf the book was on in the popular book section of Hatchards bookshop.

A sigh escaped her lips. He must have gone. The pang of

disappointment in her heart took Alice by surprise. What was it with Harry Steele?

Simple. He kissed you and you enjoyed it. And you want him to do it again. For him to touch you, to know you.

No. That was impossible. He was someone she was paying to save her sister from making a grave mistake, nothing more.

Liar.

Clutching the book, she wished to purchase to her breast, Alice turned left, intending to head to the sales counter. Her world was suddenly filled with a tall, green-eyed vision of male magnificence.

"Harry," she gasped.

He quickly backed her up against a bookshelf and murmured, "Miss North. Fancy. Meeting. You. Here."

Wicked heat pooled in her loins at the delicious way he spoke. Her nipples hardened. Whenever Harry was this close, he reduced her to a complete mush of nonsense.

Alice lifted the book and showed it to him. "Alexander Pope," she said.

He glanced at the cover. "*The Dunciad*? An interesting choice. I, myself, prefer the Marquis de Sade's poems. Especially the naughty ones. Have you read any of them?"

Alice shook her head.

Harry trailed a finger down her cheek and neck, and she shivered at his touch.

"You have to ask at the front counter for those books. They don't stock them openly on the shelves. Perhaps you and I could share an afternoon reading some of my books in the comfort of my library," he whispered.

The invitation rolled all too easily off his tongue. How many other women had been asked to spend time alone with Harry and his illicit collection of saucy poems?

"Is that how you seduce women?" she asked.

He frowned. He appeared genuinely taken aback by her words.

I've overstepped with him.

"I'm sorry. That was uncalled for," she said.

"Alice, I have never asked a lady to my home. Apart from the main drawing room where I receive clients, the rest of the house is my private sanctuary. I was offering to share it with you," he replied.

"Oh, Harry. Please forgive me." Alice went to add further to her apology, but at that moment, Harry bent and covered her lips with his own before she could muster the words. She wasn't sure if anyone heard her half-strangled cry as he grabbed her, but she honestly didn't care if they had. All that mattered was that she was once again in Harry's arms, and his tongue was in her mouth. Socially accepted norms of public behavior . . . be damned.

He took the book from her hands and set it on the shelf. The man was full of excellent ideas. With the book gone, he was able to pull her to him. Alice gasped as the hardness of his firm erection pressed against her stomach.

A woman of her station and marital status should be shocked, nay, outraged by such a thing. She should be scandalized at being handled so roughly, but all it did was make her throb in her most secret of places. Places that only she had touched in the privacy of her bed.

Her parents might well be unconventional, but they were also smart enough to have explained the birds and bees to their children as they'd stood on the cusp of adulthood. Sex was not something to be ashamed of; it was to be celebrated with a lover.

She shifted slightly against him, and Harry groaned. There was nothing else she needed to know. Harry wanted her.

He broke the kiss, sucking in deep, heavy breaths. After snatching Alice's book from the shelf, he held it in front of him. A sly grin crept to his lips. "I am shocked by your conduct, Miss North. I thought you were the prim and proper one in all this. Fancy pressing yourself against a gentleman and then kissing him in a bookshop."

She put a hand to her chest as she struggled to get her bearings. Her wits were still spinning in a circle. "Could I please have my book?"

He shook his head; the man was clearly in discomfort. "Not just yet. Give me a minute or two."

Alice stepped back, creating a respectable distance between them as another customer appeared at the end of the next aisle over. She raised an amused eyebrow at Harry but stopped when she caught a glimpse of the expression on his face. It was anything but humorous.

Oh. I see. Did I do that to him? Well now, that changes things.

"Thank you for recommending *The History of Persia*, Lord Steele. I am certain my brother shall appreciate his birthday present immensely," she said.

"It was my pleasure, Miss North. If you need me to recommend any other historical works, you only have to ask," he ground out.

The other customer continued on along the row and out of sight.

This moment was glorious in Alice's eyes. Harry had foolishly thought he had the upper hand in this little game. She might well be a novice when it came to the art of flirting, but she had still managed to teach him a nice and naughty lesson.

Alice reached out and brushed a hand on Harry's cheek. She leaned in close and touched her lips briefly to his, exalting when he swallowed deeply.

"Be careful what games you play, Lord Steele. You might find you are not always the winner," she whispered.

And with that, she snatched the book out of his hands and walked away.

Bloody. Bloody. Urgh! How was he supposed to make it all the way back to Grosvenor Street when he was in such a state? Of all the mornings he had decided to walk instead of taking his carriage. There was no way he could attempt to leave Hatchards, let alone hail a hack in his current condition.

Harry grabbed a heavy tome on global economics on his way to the back of the bookshop. With book in hand, he settled into a comfortable chair and set to dealing with the problem of his hardened member.

He was annoyed with himself. Only callow youths let their cocks run wild in public. When was the last time he had allowed a woman to get him into such an aroused state when he wasn't naked and about to engage in the sexual act?

A very long time. Never?

Opening the book at a random page, he began to read.

Capitation taxes, so far as they are levied upon the lower ranks of people, are direct taxes upon the wages of labour, and are attended with all the inconveniences of such taxes.

Within minutes, the dry notes of Adam Smith's, *The Wealth of Nations*, did the job. Harry set the book aside and turned his thoughts to the question of Alice.

He hadn't gone looking for her this morning. It had been a fortunate coincidence that she just happened to be in Hatchards at the same time he did.

The minute he'd set eyes on her, he had started to behave like a lovestruck fool—following her around the shop, hiding behind the shelves, but making sure she saw him. He sighed. It was embarrassing to think what he had done.

And all over a woman. A client.

Her reaction to his kiss was what had him truly scratching his head. There was no doubt that she enjoyed his advances; Alice had kissed him back. She hadn't even slapped him this time. He was making progress.

But progress toward what?

As Harry stepped out the front door of the bookshop, not

having purchased a single item, a spark lit in his brain. He liked Miss Alice North. She appeared to find him not completely offensive to her senses. In his part of society, marriages had been forged on less.

The thought pulled him up short. He was a clever man, but even the brightest of minds sometimes struggled to perceive what was straight in front of their faces.

On the side of the street, in the middle of the crush of Piccadilly, Lord Harry Steele grappled with the notion that perhaps he liked Alice more than just a little. He liked her a whole lot. And when he had finally wrestled the idea to the ground, he was left with one startling truth.

While he had been stealing kisses from her, Miss Alice North had stolen his heart.

Damn. I am falling for this woman.

Chapter Ten

✿

Alice waved to him from across the street.

"I am in so much trouble," he muttered as he made his way toward her.

"I was wondering how long it would take you to become presentable again," she teased.

The only polite response available to that remark, whilst one was standing in the middle of Piccadilly, was to ignore it.

Alice motioned toward a nearby carriage. "May I offer you a ride home?"

As he climbed aboard, Harry pondered when the competition between them for breaking society rules and expectations had started, because Alice seemed to be keeping up a cracking pace. He suspected she was in the lead.

The door closed behind him and he settled on the bench opposite to her.

"You are not meant to know what happens to a man who finds a woman sexually attractive. Where did the whole shy-and-naïve-miss act go?" he asked.

"You forget to whom you are talking. I don't think any of the North children were ever shy. Granted, we can be naïve at times, but my younger brother, Finn, has never been one for keeping the secrets of the world to himself. I was one of the first people he told when he'd lost his virginity," replied Alice.

He did what?

Harry blinked hard. He had to meet this Finn North and explain to him what the word *confidential* meant.

Alice rummaged around in her reticule and took out a small purse. She dangled it in front of Harry. "This is the next progress payment for your services. But I want to know what you are doing about Mister Cuthbert Saint before I hand it over."

Cheeky minx. And here was me thinking I had you in the palm of my hand.

He sensed a perceptible shift in the mood from light banter to something darker. The sexy game of hide-and seek-in the bookshop now forgotten. But if Alice was going to literally hold his money over his head, the least Harry could do was to be completely honest with her.

"We are going to wait," he replied.

'Why?" she huffed, angrily stuffing the purse back into her reticule.

Harry took in a long, slow breath, refusing to let his need for blunt cloud his judgement. He had done that once before —never again.

"There are some people working on uncovering more information. Once I am in possession of it, we can look to move forward," he said.

Harry's businesslike demeanor cracked the instant tears sprang to Alice's eyes. He leapt across the carriage and hauled her into his arms.

〜

Alice lay her head against Harry's chest and quietly sobbed. She just wanted it all to be over. For Patience to be free of

Cuthbert's hold. This waiting and taking small, measured steps was killing her. Sometimes she wished for nothing more than to strike Cuthbert down and keep hitting until there was nothing left of him.

"Why? Why does it have to be this way?" She sighed.

The stroke of his warm hand on her cheek gave little comfort. When Harry loosened the ties on her bonnet and slipped it from her head, Alice didn't protest.

"Look at me," he said.

She wiped her tears away with the heel of her hand and met his gaze.

"Not long after I started, I was dealing with a matter very similar to this one. It was early days in my scandal-managing career, and I was eager to show my client how well I could deal with the problem. I made some hasty judgements about the gentleman involved, and they were later proven to be incorrect. I didn't just tear apart a couple who were in love; I caused a man's death."

"Oh, Harry, that's terrible. But you cannot think that would happen in this case. Cuthbert doesn't love Patience," she replied.

He brushed a kiss on her forehead and ran his fingers over her hair, all the while remaining silent. Alice considered Harry's words. Could she possibly be seeing Cuthbert wrong? And what would she do if he transpired to be just as lovestruck as Patience?

I don't believe for one minute that he truly cares for her, but I would rather be sure.

She pulled out of his embrace and sat back. Harry was right to be cautious. They had to be certain and in possession of irrefutable evidence if they were going to convince Patience of the truth of Cuthbert. Her sister may eventually forgive her for unveiling him as a rascal, but she would most certainly never do that if things with Cuthbert ended in tragedy.

"How long do you think it will take?" she asked.

"A few days, possibly more. You have to trust that I have people watching him and your sister. The instant he makes a move to spirit her away, I will not hesitate to take action," replied Harry.

He took her hand in his and slipped her glove off. The soft kisses that he placed on the tip of each finger had Alice drawing a shuddering breath. It was wrong to be allowing him such liberties when they were busily trying to tear Patience and Cuthbert apart.

And yet the comfort that this unexpected tenderness brought to her was exactly what she wanted. At the onset of their relationship, they had simply flirted and teased one another. But within a short time, Harry seemed to have developed an innate understanding of what Alice needed from him. And right now, that was his strength and comfort.

"In the meantime, I want you to think about yourself. Alice, you are being so incredibly strong for both Patience and your family. But as someone who has a history of dealing with scandal, I am worried that you are in danger of becoming lost," he said.

Lost?

"When your every waking minute is spent worrying about someone else, you do lose sight of your own life. Believe me, I have seen it enough times to know when it is happening."

He had a point. Apart from the visit to the bookshop this morning, Alice couldn't remember having done anything purely for herself over the past few weeks.

"When this is all over, then I will make some time for me," she replied.

"And what about *me*? Will you have time for Harry Steele?" As he spoke, Harry moved closer. He placed the softest, most tender kiss of all time on Alice's lips. For a brief moment, everything stopped.

All the whirling thoughts in her mind slipped away,

leaving just the two of them. The only sound was the thump of her heart as it pounded in Alice's ears. She reached for his hand as he gently broke the kiss.

"Harry," she whispered.

When he came back to her, Alice met the second embrace with as much reverence as she could find in her heart.

In that moment, if he had asked her what she wanted, she would have told Harry the honest truth. She didn't want jewels or fancy clothes. She simply wanted him.

Chapter Eleven

Alice had thought that there could be nothing worse than bearing witness to Patience and Cuthbert while they cooed and made doe eyes at one another, but she was wrong. Watching them fight was torture at its worst. While Cuthbert played it cool, Patience failed to live up to her name. Tears and much wringing of handkerchiefs was the order of the evening.

"He is a beastly brute," moaned Patience. Alice simply nodded. She had learned not to offer up her true opinion of Cuthbert Saint.

What had started out as a pleasant visit to a musical event at a private home had quickly deteriorated after an argument had sprung up between Patience and Cuthbert not long after they had arrived. Cuthbert had made the critical mistake of not gushing over the new gown that Patience had debuted this evening, and her sister was making him pay dearly.

To add further to Alice's woes, she had been the one most keen to attend this particular gathering, and it had taken some kind words and a coin or two to secure an invitation. A famous conductor from Vienna was going to perform with a top-notch orchestra. After the performance, there was going to be dancing. Alice loved to dance; it was one of the few socially acceptable ways for a young woman to publicly enjoy herself within the *ton*.

"I think we should discuss this in private," said Cuthbert.

With a derisive sniff, Patience followed him to an out-of-the-way spot in the corner near one of the staircases. Alice sent a silent prayer to heaven. *Dear Lord, please let her give him his marching orders.*

"Correct me if I am wrong, but there appears to be a distinct chill between your sister and our friend tonight," said a voice from behind her.

Harry. Thank heaven for small mercies.

"Don't get your hopes up. Knowing Patience, she will forgive him, and all will be lovey-dovey before the orchestra finishes tuning their instruments." Alice cast a sideways glance at Harry as he came and stood alongside her.

When he gently placed his hand on the small of her back and left it there to linger, a shiver slid down her spine. If he had any idea what that did to her, he was keeping mum.

Alice turned and gave Harry a fuller inspection. She had never seen a man dressed in such an eye-catching color before. "Is that pink?"

Harry rolled his eyes. "Salmon, darling. I would never be so common as to wear pink. A gentleman has to have standards. I must say I love your burgundy and gold gown, especially the way you wear the sleeves off your shoulders. It suits you much better than that grey shroud you wore to the Ashton's ball."

"Um, thank you," she replied.

Alice's thoughts were too full of Harry's outfit for her to respond more than that. Her gaze roamed over his attire from top to bottom, then moved back to the top again. There was so much happening that it necessitated a second look.

He was right; the floor-length fully-buttoned-up coat was a fetching shade of salmon. So was the tall silk hat he wore.

Then came the black lace, which trimmed the cuffs of the coat and around the band of the hat. But what truly stole the show, however, was the white fur trim around the raised collar of the garment. It gave Harry's gorgeous face an almost angelic appearance.

When did I start thinking of him as being gorgeous? I have clearly lost my mind.

She caught a glimpse of bare ankle and narrowed her eyes. "Dare I ask what you are wearing beneath your outer garment?" she said.

Harry shook his head. "I don't think the hostess of this evening would forgive even me if I unbuttoned my coat. Let me just say, it is a tad daring and a whole lot scandalous."

"Why wear it, then, if you are not going to do the grand reveal?" she replied.

The slow, salacious smile which crept across his lips set her heart racing. Others might see him as bordering on lunatic, but to Alice, he was mesmerizing. Here in the middle of the toff of the *ton* was an individual who really didn't give a damn what people thought of him.

"I don't plan to stay long at this dull-as-dishwater shindy. I am here to check on our fraudulent foe and then leave," he replied.

And go where?

He was going to abandon her. Disappointment and a touch of irritation stirred within. Didn't he have any idea as to how famous this conductor was? And if not, couldn't he at least summon up enough interest in her to want to stay? Especially after the small private moments they had shared of late.

Obviously not. Foolish girl. Fancy thinking that Harry could be seriously interested in you.

That particular notion hurt Alice on a deeper level than she liked. The sting of rejection burned.

"I am sorry that you think these cultural moments are

beneath you. As for myself, I have been counting down the days until Herr Schwartz arrived in London," she bit back.

Alice turned away. Tears threatened, but Harry took hold of her arm and drew her back. Blinking hard, she glared at him. If he thought to kiss her, she was going to nip him on the lips instead. Arrogant, pompous man.

The heady scent of sandalwood soap and another mysterious spice she couldn't name quickly filled her senses. Being this close to him was like breathing in his essence.

"I'm sorry. That was cruel and unkind. I shouldn't mock something that you love. Forgive me," he said.

She had never seen Harry so earnest. There was not a trace of insincerity about him. It was tempting to ask him what had changed, but she held back.

"I never want to see you again, Cuthbert Saint. You are a . . . cold fish."

They both turned at those words. Patience came storming toward them with Cuthbert hot on her heels.

Alice put a comforting arm around her sister. "What is the matter?" she asked.

"Just a silly misunderstanding. It is nothing of consequence," replied Cuthbert, flatly.

Patience threw up her arms. "That's all I am to you—insignificant and foolish."

"You know that is not true. You mean the world to me," replied Cuthbert.

Harry caught Alice's eye, and to her bone-deep relief, he stepped forward. Patience immediately ceased her tantrum and stood staring at him, mouth agape.

"Perhaps now might be a good time to take you home, Miss Patience. My carriage is outside. I often find a little time and distance helps in these sorts of situations," offered Harry.

"Could you, Lord Steele? That would be most kind of you. We sent our carriage home, not expecting to be finished for a few hours more. What do you think, Patience?" said Alice.

Her sister pursed her lips. "I think that is very good idea. The sooner I am away from Mister Saint the better."

As Cuthbert went to protest, Harry drew him aside. "Let her go home. A good night's sleep often cures these ills."

He clearly wasn't happy with this development, but to his credit, Cuthbert didn't push the issue. He bowed to the group and quickly left.

Patience turned back to Alice and promptly burst into tears. By the time they made their exit, she was in an inconsolable state.

Harry wasted no time in having his coach brought around to the front of the elegant town house, and within minutes, the three of them were headed for Mortimer Street and the North family home.

He instructed the driver to take the carriage into the rear mews; the neighbors did not need to be granted an audience to Patience's distressed state.

A footman pulled down the steps and helped the youngest North sister to alight. Without a word of good night or gratitude, she stormed into the house, leaving an embarrassed Alice to deal with Harry.

"Thank you, Harry. You saved me from a thoroughly unpleasant evening. My sister is not one to be pacified when she is in such a mood. Mama calls her Boadicea when Patience starts getting all riled up. The only thing missing is the blue woad on her face." She rose from her seat, ready to climb out.

Harry reached over, and taking hold of the door handle, tugged it closed. He rapped on the roof, and the carriage pulled away.

The sudden jolt had a startled Alice finding herself quickly back on the bench. "Are we returning to the concert?"

"That is up to you. I know you are keen to go and listen to the orchestra, but if you are in the mood for something a little more interesting, I could take you to a place I know," he replied.

She scowled at him. Knowing Harry, *interesting* could mean a great many things. London was a city full of dark, fascinating places. A more prudent and staider woman might well have demanded he turn the carriage around and take her home. Alice North was fast discovering that she wasn't that kind of woman.

Still, she wasn't going to go quietly.

"Is this *place* that you speak of somewhere that I am going to be able to tell my sister or parents about?"

Harry moved and came to sit alongside her. He took hold of her hand. "Let's just say I don't think it is somewhere that you would wish to speak of in polite company. But it is a place where you and I *need* to go."

"I haven't lived as sheltered a life as you seem to think," she replied.

He brushed a kiss on her lips. She met his gaze. A bright impish light glowed in his clear green eyes. "Alice, my sweet, you have not seen more than an inch of London. Your parents might well have led you to believe you were living a free life, but in truth, they just gave you a bigger cage."

She didn't like hearing him say this. Alice had always felt she and her siblings had been granted freedoms beyond the norm. That the North family was somehow special.

"My family don't keep their women in cages," she replied.

"No? Just because you cannot see the sides of it doesn't mean that it is not there. Come with me tonight. Allow yourself to experience things you have never done before, then tell me how much your life is not your own."

Who knew what danger Harry might expose her to this night, or what tomorrow morning would look like through her eyes? He frightened her; she wasn't ashamed to admit that to herself. But he also tempted her, challenged the way she saw things and what her heart desired for the future.

If there was a chance that Harry could be the one man in all of London who not only wanted her for himself, but who she could possibly share her heart with, she owed it to herself to take the risk. "Promise you will do all you can to keep me safe tonight. I am trusting you, Harry."

He slipped his hand around Alice's waist and pressed himself against her. She searched his gaze, and for just the tiniest of moments, she could have sworn she saw love staring back.

Harry Steele and love. Oh, Alice, you are headed into treacherous waters. Be careful.

"I will always protect you. Where we are going is somewhere, I hope you will feel free to be the real Alice North," he said.

Alice nodded. She could only pray that if tonight did reveal the truth of who she was, Harry would still want her. If he didn't, she may as well stay in that cage.

Chapter Twelve

Lord Harry Steele had done some really stupid things in his life. He'd engaged in downright dangerous activities, which had brought him to the brink of death more than once. Taking Alice to a secret London sex club was right up there with the best or worst of his choices.

He was already having second thoughts by the time the carriage pulled into the rear mews of a plain brick building in Jermyn Street. No one was foolish enough to enter the Temple of Diana by way of the front entrance.

When the club's footman opened the carriage door, Harry waved him away. "Give us a minute, Janus, will you?"

Janus politely backed away and stood out of earshot. The staff at this establishment were well-trained in protecting their clients' privacy.

Harry paused for a moment in an attempt to collect his thoughts. Bringing Alice to one of London's notorious sex clubs was a risk. If she didn't take it the way he hoped she would, it was more than likely any possible chance he had for winning her heart would be left stone dead.

"What is it?" she asked.

"Inside that building is a club called the Temple of Diana.

It is full of men and women who have escaped their cages and embraced who they are; I want you to see them because that is the world to which I belong."

Alice frowned, and Harry inwardly cursed himself for having put their relationship in peril. He waited. Any moment now, she would ask him to take her home and not to make mention of this night ever again. His greatest fear was that if she did just that, the growing connection between them would fracture and die.

Can you blame her?

"I see. But why have you brought me here? I am not of your world," she replied.

Harry swallowed deeply. A wrong word or poorly put phrase and it could all be over between them before it had begun. "What if you were of my world—if, for a time, our lives were somehow bound together? Wouldn't you want to know as much of me as you could? Because if we are to truly discover whatever this thing is between us, you need to understand who I am."

Silence reigned once more. Alice turned her gaze from him to the fancy gold-tasseled trim of the curtains. She lifted a hand to them, running her fingers along their finely tailored edge. The tassels connected and released with her touch. "Yes, I would."

And with that, Alice reached for the door. Harry followed; his heart thumping so hard in his chest that it echoed in his ears.

Nothing ventured, nothing gained.

꽃

The door which led into the Temple of Diana was plain black with a simple silver handle. Nothing denoted its purpose or what lay beyond.

As they drew close to the entrance, following the burly

thug-cum-footman, Harry took a firm grip of Alice's hand. "You will see things that you didn't know existed. And for those that already did, your perception of them will be changed forevermore. There are only two things I ask of you tonight. One, that you keep an open mind."

Alice huffed at him in annoyance. She hated being patronized. "And two?"

"You don't run screaming from the place. Some of these people are my closest friends."

She was about to enquire as to why she would do such a thing when the door was opened, and Harry hauled her inside.

They walked down a long dark hallway. Every step had her heart thumping and her mouth as dry as a desert. At the end of the hall, in front of a gold draped curtain, stood another footman. This servant was dressed in black from head to toe. He reminded her of the butler at Harry's house. Perhaps this was where he obtained his servants.

The footman bowed low. "Lord Steele, always a pleasure."

His gaze then fell on Alice. It lingered, roaming seductively over her body. Under her cloak, Alice shivered. She was still fully dressed, but somehow, he had managed to make her feel completely naked.

Harry handed his hat to the footman. "Hypnos, good to see you."

Hypnos. Janus. Temple of Diana. All the staff are named after Greek gods.

Harry didn't introduce her to Hypnos, instead he slipped his hands to the clasp of her cloak and unfastened it. Alice shrugged out of it, and with elegant ceremony, Harry handed it to the footman. Harry then unbuttoned his long salmon-colored coat.

Alice bit down on her bottom lip as he rid himself of the coat and turned to her. Now she understood why Harry had been reluctant to take it off at the earlier function.

He was clad in, of all things, a short, gold-trimmed toga. It reached just below his knee, leaving his calves on full display.

What the devil?

"Temple of Diana. One must pay suitable homage to the gods," he said.

Alice was too busy staring at Harry's shapely legs to take in much for the next few minutes. The footman drew back the curtain and ushered them through.

They stepped into a sensual wonderland that could have easily come from ancient mythology. She stood blinking for a moment, unsure of where to look, or whether she should avert her gaze entirely.

In a large room, which Alice surmised had once been a ballroom, several dozen people were gathered. It was what they were wearing and doing that left her speechless.

There were a few men dressed similarly to Harry in short, linen togas—a number of which barely covered their buttocks. Others wore evening gowns matched with white gloves and shawls.

Men dressed as women. I have never seen that before.

Harry slipped his arm around her waist and murmured, "Let your eyes take it all in, but don't allow your mind to judge. All of these people have embraced their natures, but society sees them as a potential threat. This is a place where they can be safe to express themselves, to be happy."

Alice's gaze drifted from the first group as some female guests arrived from another room into the main space. She blinked as she took in what they were wearing. It was very little. All were bare-breasted. One was fully naked; she was also painted silver from head to toe.

Low sofas and couches were dotted around the room. On them sat couples engaged in various different amorous pursuits. She put a hand to her lips as a woman straddled a naked man and sunk onto him.

Why is this making me so hot and my core pulse?

Harry motioned to a nearby footman bearing a tray of drinks. "Two brandies, thank you."

With shaking hands, Alice accepted her glass. Without even looking at it, she took a sip. It was strong and bitter. Holding the brandy out in front of her, she studied it before offering it back to him. "I have never drunk brandy before. People always say it is not meant for women."

Harry shook his head and refused to take the drink. He pointed at the glass. "Have some more. Remember that cage you keep telling yourself you don't live in?"

Another footman stopped in front of them. He held a tray, on which was a selection of cigars.

Harry took a moment, then selected a thin cigar, which the footman lit and handed to him. He raised it to his lips and drew back deeply before blowing a long thin wisp of grey smoke into the air.

Alice was unsure as to whether she was game to try it if Harry offered. The brandy and the scenery were already going to her head.

"Relax. I am not going to offer you hashish. I want your thoughts to be clear for the rest of the evening. You won't be getting high tonight. Another time perhaps," said Harry.

He guided her toward a nearby staircase and they slowly began to ascend. When they reached the first landing, they stopped. Alice set her brandy glass on a nearby side table before taking in the gathering below; Harry came to stand close behind her.

"Take your time. Look closely at what is happening. Tell me how it affects you. Does it stir desires deep within or are you simply shocked?" he said.

Her gaze roamed over the scene below. Men kissing one another. Women on their knees in front of seated men, their heads bobbing up and down. A room full of people exploring their sexual desires.

She gasped. On a long table lay a woman completely

naked; two men ran their hands and mouths over her body. Even from this distance, the woman's groans of pleasure could be heard.

A soft kiss was brushed on the side of Alice's neck.

"What does it do to you? Tell me."

She was tight and throbbing in places that ached for his touch. For a moment, she imagined herself being the woman on the table, with Harry's lips on her heated skin. Of him bringing forth her own cries and sobs of completion.

"I know I should think all this is utterly scandalous, but for some reason I don't. I just can't put anything I am experiencing right now into words," she murmured.

He blew a soft, heated kiss in her ear and she swallowed deeply. Desire thrummed through her. Dangerous. Needy. *Harry*.

"Would you prefer to show me?"

She nodded.

He slipped his hand into hers and drew her away from the edge of the landing and up a shorter flight of stairs. At the top, they turned and headed along a narrow hallway which had doors to the left and right. Harry's steps didn't falter; he seemed to know exactly where he was going.

Five doors down on the left, he stopped. "Whatever happens in this room, you are in control. If at any time you wish me to stop, you only have to say the word. If I do anything that you don't like, I will cease it immediately. Nothing happens without your express consent. Do you understand?"

"Yes."

He led her into the room and locked the door behind them. Alice suddenly wished she hadn't left her brandy behind. She was in need of a stiff drink.

Why is this so wrong and yet it feels so right?

On a low table various bottles of wine and champagne were set. Harry had said he wanted her clearheaded for this evening, but she would dearly love to take the edge off her passions. She fought off the lure of alcohol, knowing that it was the one thing she could resist. Her body craved a hundred other heated temptations.

Harry crushed the end of the cannabis cigar into a nearby glass ashtray, then returned to Alice's side. He pulled her to him and captured her mouth in a scorching kiss. Lips and tongues met in a now familiar dance. When Harry groaned into her mouth, Alice's core clenched once more.

She wanted this man, ached to have his hands on her naked body. To let him do to her whatever he wanted. To give and be possessed.

Nimble fingers made quick work of the laces on her gown before tugging the front of her bodice open and pushing the sides down. He frowned at her undergarments.

"Tut-tut, Alice. A light corset? I would have thought you would go for the French fashion and wear nothing under your gown," he teased.

She drew in a shaky breath and tried to steady her nerves. "Yes, well this is England and it is early December. This gown is chilly enough. The corset helps bridge the gap between being fashionable and warm."

So much for being a sexual siren.

From inside his boot, Harry produced a small knife. He gripped the top of Alice's stiff undergarment and grinned. "I hope you have plenty of these at home. May I?"

Harry's knife was pointed at the laces. She gave a moment's brief pause, then nodded.

With a deft flick of the blade, he cut the front of her corset straight down the middle, all the way to her waist. Without hesitation, Harry pushed the two halves apart and bared Alice's breasts.

She gasped. "Oh."

Cool air kissed her nipples, instantly turning them to hard pebbles. Before she had time to fully absorb the shock of being semi-naked in front of him, Harry had laid his hand on one of her breasts, resting it in his palm. His thumb gently rubbed back and forth over her peaked nipple.

"May I?" he asked again.

She wasn't entirely sure what he was asking this time, but she nodded anyway. The way lust was coursing through her body, she didn't have the willpower to say no.

Bending, he took the rosy bud between his teeth and gently nipped. It sent a powerful shockwave through her body. "Oh god," she moaned.

As he proceeded to lick, suck, and nip at first one breast, and then the other, Alice was left struggling for air. With her hands resting on his shoulders, she was at his mercy. An ever-growing need for release slowly built as Harry inflicted a masterful, exquisite torture on her body. Heat pooled in her core and her clit throbbed.

When he finally released her from his attentions, Alice whimpered.

Why did you have to stop?

With her hand in his, Harry led Alice over to a nearby low sofa. When he had arranged her with her back against it, he took her lips once more in a soft, tender kiss. She sensed his hard erection poking against her stomach, and the memory of the woman downstairs with her lover's cock in her mouth suddenly filled Alice's mind.

Will he want me to do that to him? He will have to teach me.

"Are you ready for more?" he asked.

This game of sexual manners was exactly what he had promised. Nothing happened without her express approval.

"Yes."

He slid a hand beneath her skirts, tracing his thumb up the inside of her thigh. When he touched the tip of her sex, he stopped. Alice whimpered with need.

"May I?"

"I shall die if you don't" she replied.

And with that, he slipped his thumb into her wet heat and began to stroke. Each time he withdrew to the edge of release, his knuckle rubbed over her sensitive bud and she sobbed.

"Harry."

Harder and deeper he stroked her, creating an urgent need which built steadily within. Between her sobs and groans, all Alice could do was let Harry take the lead. She was completely at his mercy.

"You saw the woman on the table being pleasured by a man's mouth. Did it arouse you?" he murmured.

"Yes."

"May I?"

She had got in enough of an aroused state simply watching from the top of the landing. The prospect of Harry doing that to her had Alice sucking in a shuddering breath.

"Please," she whispered.

He drew her onto the carpet, then knelt between her legs. The instant his tongue touched her oversensitive nib, her hips bucked. A wicked chuckle echoed in the quiet space. The rogue knew how close she was to exploding.

"Harry," she begged.

He answered her plea with his thumb and mouth, thrusting into her sex while he licked and sucked at her clitoris. She grasped for him, her fingers spearing into his hair.

Tension throbbed through her body. She was desperate to reach that final climax. After tearing his mouth away, Harry rose over Alice and thrust two fingers deep into her heat. He continued to run his thumb around the edge of her bud, teasing cries and groans from her.

She met his gaze, hungry and urgent. It was as if his green eyes had turned ablaze. The passion on his face was breathtaking.

"Come for me, Alice. Break free of that cage and embrace who you are."

"Kiss me," she demanded.

He wiped his face on the edge of her torn corset, then captured her lips. As his tongue pressed into her mouth, his fingers thrust deep into her sex. Alice clutched at the soft linen of Harry's ridiculous toga, tearing it between her fingers as she sought to find purchase in the swirling maelstrom.

One hard, final thrust pushed her over the edge. She came hard, screaming. "Harry!"

He kissed her once more, while continuing to stroke her as she lowered from her climax. Her whole body still thrummed with pleasure.

"Good girl. Now you get champagne," he murmured.

He got to his feet, leaving Alice lying on the floor. For a time, she lay staring up at the ornate cornice which edged the cream-colored ceiling, her heart still thumping hard in her chest. She had just had her first orgasm with a man, and it had been stupendous.

Her brain, meanwhile, was still trying to make sense of it all. Of where she was and with whom. A matter of days ago, she only knew Lord Harry Steele by word of his reputation. And now . . . well, *that* had just happened.

When her orgasm-scrambled mind finally took in her surroundings once more, Alice sat up. Across at the table, Harry was busy pouring champagne into a glass.

"I think I may have to hide this corset from my maid. She might ask questions as to what happened to it," she said.

He wandered back over to her and helped Alice to her feet. "I could explain it to her if you like. Or you could just leave it here."

She returned his cheeky grin with a soft chortle. The less any of the North family servants knew about her secret, scandalous life, the better. There was already more than enough explaining to be done when her parents returned to England.

With champagne glasses in hand, they settled onto the

sofa. Harry drew Alice into his arms, brushing a kiss on her forehead.

"I'm proud of you tonight. You stayed when many other women would not have done so. And you shared a part of yourself with me that honestly leaves me humbled."

This evening had been one of many revelations. She had placed her trust in Harry and allowed herself to come under his careful loving. What she had learned about herself and her desires, however, would take some careful thought and reflection.

Alice had an ever-growing list of questions to ask Harry about his life, but now didn't seem the right time. They had shared an intimate moment, one where she had offered her body to him freely.

She didn't want to think about how many other women he had brought to this place. Nor which of them had also fallen to Harry's tempting touch and foolishly offered him their hearts.

Here am I trying to save Patience from making a stupid mistake, and yet I could be doing something even worse.

The irony of the situation was all too clear.

"What happens now?" She left it an open-ended question, allowing Harry to decide the direction his answer would take.

"We finish our champagne, and I take you home. As for our friend, Mister Saint, I am expecting some reports to arrive tomorrow regarding him and his provenance. Once I have those, we should make some decisions. I have a feeling time may not be on our side," he said.

Alice pulled out of Harry's embrace and sat up, setting her champagne glass on the floor. She pulled the ripped corset free and set it aside. Here seemed as good a place as any to abandon it. She began to work the laces of her gown as best she could. Focusing on dressing seemed the best response to her disappointment at him failing to mention either them or what had just occurred.

Perhaps he is angry. Was he expecting me to pleasure him? Of course, he was.

She turned and laid a hand softly on his knee, brushing her fingers up and down.

His hand stilled hers. "No. Now is not the time."

"You don't want me to do anything for you?" she asked.

He shook his head. "The only thing I want you to give me is not mine to claim. Only the man you choose to marry has such a right."

Alice withdrew her hand. Harry's words were clear enough. He was prepared to take their sexual relationship only so far. Anything that would compel him into making an offer of marriage to her was not a part of those plans.

He did say we might be a part of each other's lives for a time. He didn't say forever.

"Would you please take me home?" she asked.

She chided herself for being foolish enough to allow her growing crush on him to whisper promises of a future—the only solace being that Harry at least had the good sense to know where to draw the line.

If he had asked 'May I?' I might have said yes. Thank god he didn't.

To a man like Harry, Miss Alice North was likely nothing more than just another interesting diversion—one of many in his colorful, scandalous world.

The sooner they had the matter of Cuthbert Saint sorted, the quicker she could conclude her contract with Lord Harry Steele and be out of his life. He would go on to his next client, and she would be left to tend to her wounded heart.

Foolish girl. Perhaps you are better off in your cage.

Chapter Thirteen

❦

"Where did you get to last evening?" asked George.

Harry gave a disinterested shrug. "Out and about." He wasn't going to make mention of Alice or their visit to the Temple of Diana. Fortunately, the club was one with strict rules regarding discretion. Names were never spoken outside of its walls. Many of Harry's former clients were members, and he knew enough dirty secrets about them to be confident that his visit would not be mentioned by anyone.

They were waiting at the RR Coaching Company offices for Stephen and Monsale to arrive with news of Cuthbert Saint. Harry's mood was dark. The three cups of black tea—no lemon, no milk, no honey—which he had already downed this morning had done nothing to lighten his spirits.

Perhaps I should have begun the morning with whisky. Start as you mean to go on.

George frowned at him. If anyone could read people as well as Harry, it was the master thief. "You are certainly Lord Misery Guts this morning. Maybe I don't want to know where you went last night."

"It's not that. Things in this case have become a little

complicated. And then there is the question of Milton," replied Harry.

"The piglet? What's wrong with him?"

"Papa's breeding manager sent word that he needs Milton in the country," he replied.

All his life, even after he and his father had fallen out, Harry had taken care of the youngest male breeding pigs for the Steele family estate. From the time the piglets were weaned off their mother, to the time they were put to stud, they were Harry's to care for and feed.

George sighed. This wasn't the first time any of Harry's friends had been forced to give him sympathy over a curly tailed piglet. "You do know he is going off to the country to live a life that few humans, let alone animals, ever get to enjoy? Eating, sleeping, and fucking. Where do I sign up?"

Talk of Milton kept the subject of Alice North at bay; she was the real reason for his melancholy mood. Last night had been magical. The expression of joy on her face as he'd brought her to completion had gone straight to his heart.

And then she'd cried out his name. *Harry.* A man would have to be made of stone not to fall in love with a woman right at that moment.

But you were already in danger of falling. Holding her just tipped you over.

Any thought of not getting involved with Alice North had long ago gone up in flames. He wanted her, body and soul.

The only thing which had held him back last night and stopped him from asking 'May I?' was that he'd known to his bones that she would have said yes. And he would not have been able to resist.

Saving Patience North from one imprudent marriage while luring her sister into another would defy all the laws of irony and logic.

If she is to be yours, you have to offer her everything. And that includes the truth.

The thought of telling Alice about the RR Coaching Company and its dubious business enterprises made Harry's mouth go dry. Coming from new money, she must already know what it was like to be treated as someone less than equal by London high society. What was the chance that she would choose him if she knew that being a part of his life would mean accepting that her husband was regularly involved in shady and downright illegal dealings?

Would she take that risk, knowing that if things ever went awry, her reputation would be destroyed?

The thunder of boots on wooden stairs heralded the arrival of Sir Stephen Moore and The Duke of Monsale. Harry was grateful for the interruption. The question of Alice and any possible future with her had kept him awake all through the night.

"Ah, just the man we want," said Monsale.

Harry moved away from where he and George had both been toasting their asses in front of the fire. After the long chilly walk up from the River Thames, a few minutes of buttock warming was always in order at this time of the year.

"We have news," announced Stephen.

Monsale tossed a leather pouch onto the long wooden table, before heading over to the nearby sideboard on which a platter of various meats and some cold roast potatoes sat. Stephen followed him, grabbing two plates from off the table as he went. His gaze went to the fireside and he grinned as Harry wriggled his backside.

"Cuthbert Saint is no saint. Never went to Eton. In fact, there is no record of him anywhere. The man does not exist," added Stephen.

"But . . ." said Monsale, with a raise of his eyebrows.

Harry's ears pricked up. Monsale always proceeded the juicy, noteworthy bits of any investigation or scandal with that tantalizing word. He and Stephen exchanged a grin.

"What we do have is a missing valet. A chap by the name

of Cuthbert Leigh who used to work for a Scottish family just across the border. Disappeared about six months ago after having helped himself to a number of valuable pieces of plate and jewelry belonging to his employer. The description of this Cuthbert matches the blackguard we have been following here in London."

All the fragments of the picture slowly drew closer together. The man who knew how to treat champagne stains had been a valet. And they now knew the origin of the expensive trinkets Cuthbert had pawned at Jones and Son.

"Good, so we are pretty confident we have the make of him. Now I have to decide what to do about getting him away from Patience North," said Harry.

Time was of paramount importance. Notwithstanding the fight that the two of them had had the previous evening, Harry suspected there was every chance that matters between Alice's sister and Cuthbert would be back on even keel quickly. With Cuthbert's coin becoming low, he would likely do everything he had to in order to be able to make a move with Alice's sister.

"I need to speak with my client this morning. Inform her of these developments and get her approval to make the next move," he said.

Monsale's brows knitted together in a worried expression. He wasn't one for ever asking a woman her opinion. The fact that he was still unwed at the age of one and thirty probably had something to do with his inability to sweet-talk the ladies.

"Why are you asking a prim little miss for her thoughts?" asked Monsale.

George cleared his throat in an obvious attempt to stifle a laugh. Stephen, meanwhile, studied the platter of meats as if it held the secret to life and the universe.

"Because, your grace, she is paying me. And I actually value her opinion when it comes to her sister. She is the one who is going to have to mop up the mess after all this is over. I would prefer it if the pile of shit she has to clean is as small as possible," replied Harry.

"Bah!" huffed Monsale.

Harry picked up the satchel and made for the stairs. If he moved quickly enough and went back to Grosvenor Street, he could track Alice down this morning. "Thank you. This gives me all that I need to move on our friend Cuthbert. I shall send word again to our people in Gretna letting them know that a possible elopement may be imminent."

"Send word if you need help!" cried George.

As he hurried to the rear mews and summoned the stable boy to fetch his horse, Harry took the opportunity to gather his thoughts. *How am I to deal with this blackguard and cause the least amount of damage?*

Publicly unmasking Cuthbert could be problematic, as it could also expose Harry to scrutiny. His carefully crafted foppish personae had taken a long time to build. He wasn't going to risk it just for the sake of expediency.

Harry wasn't a man with a penchant for violence, so having Cuthbert roughed up and left for dead would never be his first choice. Nor would any attempt to have him arrested be likely to succeed. Without the victim of the theft being able to bring charges, the authorities would have nothing to go on, and Harry was not going to risk Cuthbert facing the hangman over a few pieces of jewelry.

He slipped a coin into the stable boy's hand and took the reins of his horse. Apart from trying to talk Patience out of continuing to see Cuthbert Saint, there was really only one other sensible option left.

"If it has to be, it has to be," he muttered.

All he had to do was to get Alice to appreciate the value of a firmly worded threat delivered at gunpoint.

Chapter Fourteen

"Isn't it divine? He is so thoughtful."

Alice swallowed the last of her breakfast and followed it with a gulp of tea. Listening to Patience carrying on over the bracelet that Cuthbert had sent as an apology would make anyone struggle to eat their food.

Her sister waved the trinket in Alice's face and she was forced to paint a smile on her lips in response. "Yes, it is pretty."

It was also cheaply made and would probably turn Patience's wrist green before the day was out. Not that she would either notice or care. What likely mattered more to Patience was that Cuthbert had thoughtfully chosen a bracelet the same color as the new gown over which he and she had fought.

After the less-than-satisfactory end to the evening with Harry last night, Alice didn't feel up to playing the role of happy big sister this morning. Her heart ached too much.

Seeing Patience gush over a man who could only bring her misery compounded her own sense of sadness.

"I wonder if Cuthbert is going to be at any social gatherings this evening. I really should seek him out and give him my thanks. Mama always says you should do everything to help smooth over tiffs with your spouse," said Patience.

The mere mention of Cuthbert and spouse in the same breath had Alice wishing she hadn't bothered with that second piece of pork pie. A knock at the door of the breakfast room stopped Alice from saying what she really thought of the idea of being related to Cuthbert Saint.

Knowing her stubborn sister, if Alice said anything against him, Patience would start making plans to have the banns read.

The North family butler entered carrying a silver tray, upon which sat a note. Alice silently prayed.

Please. Please. Please, let it be a letter from Mama and Papa saying they are on their way home to England.

If it were, she might still have a chance to convince her sister that any possible talk of marriage could wait until Cuthbert was able to speak with their father.

She took the note and quickly read it.

Developments on CS. Come to Grosvenor Street this morning. H.

The man was nothing if not succinct with his words.

If the note had not made mention of Cuthbert, she would have been tempted to ignore Harry's request. Instead she folded the paper and put it in her pocket.

After downing the last of her tea, Alice rose from the table. "I have to go out this morning. Let's discuss our evening plans when I return."

If Harry was looking to make a move on Cuthbert, she didn't want to be caught wrong-footed at any social event. Keeping her sister away from being connected with a scandal was crucial.

Half an hour later, Alice knocked on the front door of number 16 Grosvenor Street. Harry's dark-clothed hulk of a butler answered the door, but this time she pushed past him and made for the stairs, leaving him to follow in her wake.

She found Harry standing by the window in the drawing room; the piglet was nowhere to be seen.

"Miss Alice North," announced the butler.

Harry nodded at him. "Alice, this is Sir Stephen Moore. He has been working with me on the case. Stephen is involved in the coaching company which I partly own."

Stephen bowed low. "At your service, Miss North."

"Service? Is that what you call answering the door rudely, not showing a lady to a chair, and generally doing a terrible job of being a butler?" she replied.

He chuckled. "Yes, sorry about that. The first morning you came here, I wasn't in the best of moods. You are not the only one with family problems."

She took the seat he offered, privately relieved when Stephen came and sat next to her. The last thing Alice wanted this morning was to be alone with Harry. The man himself strolled over to the center of the room and stood in front of a low coffee table, facing her.

"You sent word that you had new information about Cuthbert." Keeping her gaze firmly fixed on Harry, she pretended not to notice the look which passed between him and Stephen. She wasn't here for niceties; she was here for answers.

Harry cleared his throat. "Yes, we can confirm that Cuthbert did not attend Eton. We also have solid evidence that his name is in fact Cuthbert Leigh, and that until a matter of months ago, he was employed as a valet for a wealthy Scottish family. He has been funding his stay in London with the proceeds from the sale of items he stole from them."

Alice clapped her hands together. This was the news she had been waiting to hear. Confirmation that Cuthbert was a fortune-hunting blackguard who only wanted to win the love of her sister in order to get his hands on her dowry.

"So, what now?" she replied.

"Eager little thing," murmured Stephen.

She shot him a disdainful look. "It's not your sister who is in grave danger of being married to a rogue, so perhaps you might want to shut your mouth."

"Steady on!" replied Stephen.

Alice reached into her reticule and pulled out the coin purse. She stood and tossed it onto the table in front of Harry. "According to the contract, that is the penultimate payment. I am paying for your services, Lord Steele. It is high time you delivered."

Harry glanced at the purse but left it where it had landed. He and Alice locked gazes; she flinched when she caught sight of the expression on his face. She had fully expected to see open defiance and was surprised that instead it was a mixture of hurt and confusion.

You cannot be that clueless about how I would take your words last night. You expect me to come out of my cage while you lurk behind the door of your stone castle.

She dropped her gaze to the Persian rug on the floor as anger and disappointment battled.

"Alice, could we please fill you in on the plan and get your approval?" said Harry.

She nodded, grateful that he was making some effort toward showing her at least a modicum of respect.

"A ticket will be sent to Cuthbert Saint at the Grand Hotel today inviting him to join you and Patience at the theatre this evening. This, of course, is merely a ruse to make sure that we know where he will be at that time," said Harry.

"Not long after he leaves the hotel, he will find himself having a little chat with a gentleman dressed all in black. The pistol in his face should help convince him that he needs to quit his accommodations and depart London forthwith," added Stephen.

"And you will send word once the message has been delivered?" she asked.

"Of course," replied Harry.

Alice nodded at the purse. "Once you provide me with confirmation that Cuthbert Saint has indeed left town, I shall pay the remainder of your fee. Good day to you, gentlemen."

Without a second glance, she headed for the door. Alice was downstairs and out into the street before the tears finally got the better of her. After all that she thought she had felt for Harry Steele, the only emotion left this morning was humiliation.

In a matter of hours, she would hopefully be rid of Cuthbert Saint. And with the end of their contract, Harry would also be gone. Only then could she start to find a way to get him out of her heart.

˚

"What happened to the sweet romance that was bubbling between the two of you?" asked Stephen.

Harry picked up the coin purse and tucked it into his jacket pocket. All night, he had lain awake and worried as to whether he had made a grave mistake in taking Alice to the Temple of Diana. Wondering if perhaps she had simply got caught up in the moment, and then once the haze of lust had cleared her mind, regret had swooped in.

"I have a horrible feeling that I may have pushed Alice North too far out of her area of comfort, and she is now in retreat. All I can focus on right this minute is Cuthbert Saint. If we succeed in frightening him off tonight, then maybe I will be able to address the matter of the two of us and whether we could have a future," he replied.

Stephen got to his feet and came to Harry's side, placing a brotherly pat on his shoulder. "This was always going to be a problem for us rogues when it came to be taking on wives. Harry, you have to succeed with Alice, because if you don't then what hope do the rest of us have? Not that I plan to ever enter into the unholy mess of matrimony."

Harry nodded. Apart from Stephen's foolish aversion to marriage, he was right. Of all the members of the RR Coaching Company, Harry was the one with the most legitimate career. Angus and George were respectively, smugglers and thieves. Stephen specialized in acts of revenge. And Monsale was up to his elbows in every money-making scheme in the country, with a penchant for the illegal ones.

It was going to take a great deal of love and understanding on the part of any woman to sign up to a life with a husband who lived a secret life outside of the law.

The cold and distant way Alice had been with him this morning didn't fill Harry with any sense of hope.

Damn.

He pushed the worry of Alice to the back of his mind as best he could. He and Stephen had a job to do. "Go and get your pistol. I will organize the theatre ticket. Let's handle what we can tonight, and I will deal with the rest later."

For a long while after Stephen had left the room, he pondered his predicament. Tell Alice everything and hope that she might feel enough affection for him to consider becoming his wife. That would mean her having to accept some hard truths about him and his friends.

The other option was for him to permanently step away from the illegal operations of the RR Coaching Company and try to eke out an honest living. To give up on his friends.

Bloody hell, what am I going to do?

There was one thing he was sure of right at this moment; he couldn't build a future with Alice based on a lie.

She is an heiress; her dowry must be substantial. You could live off her father's money.

"No. That would make me no better than Cuthbert Saint. And she would hate me."

Chapter Fifteen

❦

A little before seven o'clock that evening, Cuthbert Saint left the Grand Hotel and started on the short walk to Drury Lane Theatre. He made it as far as Broad Court.

Passing number 15 Broad Court, he was suddenly grabbed from behind and dragged off the street and through a doorway. The door was firmly closed, and he was left standing in a foyer lit only by a small chandelier.

"You've picked the wrong gentleman to rob. I have no money," he pleaded.

From out of the dark, a large figure, clad all in black appeared. He walked with measured steps, oozing menace. Harry, who was standing well out of sight in a corner, slowly shook his head. Stephen had a thing for dramatic effect.

"I know exactly who you are, Cuthbert Leigh. And what you are up to," said Stephen.

A satisfying gasp came from their prisoner. Harry much preferred that to the haughty scoff which professional villains deemed as the hallmark of their trade.

"What do you want?" replied Cuthbert.

Stephen cocked his pistol and raised it, aiming straight for

Cuthbert's face. If he fired now, the shot would be at near point-blank range and most certainly fatal.

"You give up on trying to win Patience North's hand and you leave London. Tonight. If you don't then my friends and I will make sure you are the victim of a terrible accident."

If it didn't put his whole career in jeopardy, Harry would be the one holding the pistol. But a mask and a black suit couldn't hide a man's voice. He dared not risk Cuthbert recognizing him.

"But I love Patience. I wish to marry her," replied Cuthbert.

The man had balls; he wasn't going to take the threat at face value. He had more spine that Harry had expected him to possess.

"Have you asked yourself whether she cares for you? Who else do you think sent me?" snorted Stephen.

He retrieved a coin purse from his coat pocket and threw it to Cuthbert, who quickly caught it.

"There is enough money in that purse to get you a start anywhere else in the country. Though I would suggest you might want to forget about the north. There is a Scottish lord who might be very interested in your whereabouts and also that of some of his trinkets," said Stephen.

Even in the poor light, Harry caught a glimpse of the shock on Cuthbert's face. He clearly hadn't been expecting anyone to know about his past life.

His head and shoulders dropped, and for the briefest of moments, Harry felt a twinge of pity. That could very well be him standing there while a stranger threatened to unveil his secret life.

Remember what you said to Alice. Steady your nerves.

"Alright, I will leave London. If Patience does not want me, then I will go," said Cuthbert.

"Good man. In time, you will see that you have made the right decision. Now, you and I are going to leave by the rear entrance where a carriage is waiting. The late mail coach to Harwich leaves from the Spread Eagle Coaching Company in Gracechurch Street in an hour. I intend that you will be on board. My loaded pistol will make certain of it."

Cuthbert closed his eyes and sighed. "I did love her. Could you please at least let Patience know that she held my heart?"

Bloody hell. Just go! Leave the poor girl in peace.

Harry moved farther into the shadows as Stephen guided Cuthbert out the door, only slightly relaxing as the sound of the lock clicking reverberated in the silence.

As soon as he had heard from Stephen that Cuthbert Saint had indeed boarded the coach to the English coast, he would send word to Alice. The job was done.

As he made his way back out into Broad Court, Harry had a sinking feeling that the easy part was now over, but what lay ahead may well be out of his control.

Chapter Sixteen

❦

Alice replied by letter early the next morning thanking Harry for his efforts but left it at that. A second note had reached the house late last night. He may well have quit London, but Cuthbert Saint had not gone quietly.

"He says he has to leave for a time but begged me not to forget about him. Oh, Alice, what could possibly have happened?" said Patience.

They were in the drawing room of their home in Mortimer Street, midmorning, neither having got much sleep. Patience had stayed up until the early hours crying, and Alice had sat beside her on the sofa, silently holding her hand.

In the hour after dawn, Patience had gone for a walk around the block to get some fresh air. When she returned, Alice was relieved to see that her sister had dried her tears and seemed a little more at peace.

You knew this moment was always coming; you just have to get through today. Give it time. She will forget Cuthbert Saint and find someone else suitable.

Alice schooled her features into the best placid expression she could muster. Her sister wasn't a fool, and if she gave the merest hint of having been involved in the sudden departure of Cuthbert, Patience would surely know.

"Perhaps he has family obligations. Or even a new position to take up. Who knows? Men can be such fickle creatures," she replied.

"It was all so sudden. One moment we were talking about visiting the theatre, the next he was gone," said Patience.

"Well perhaps the best thing you can do right now is to get on with your life and await his next letter. If Mister Saint is true, then he will write."

Shut up, Alice. What are you saying? Don't encourage her to carry a torch. Oh, I wish Harry were here. He is so much better at this lying lark than I am.

She hadn't seen him since the previous day at Grosvenor Street with Sir Stephen Moore, and her mind kept returning to the night prior at the Temple of Diana. To what Harry and she had shared.

Patience wasn't the only North sister wondering where a man was, and whether he wanted a future with her. Harry Steele was constantly in her thoughts.

The prospect of spending the next few days at home while they both stewed over men didn't fill her with any sense of joy. A fun diversion was what was needed. "How about we get our things and head out to Oxford Street this morning? I have some Christmas shopping to do, and I'm sure you could do with a spot of fresh air. Then, tonight, we should find ourselves a nice party to attend and try to catch up with friends."

She was tired, and a small headache sat behind her right eye, but Alice was determined not to succumb to the situation. Anything was preferable to sitting at home and wondering.

"I suppose you are right," replied Patience with a resigned sigh.

Alice rose from her place on the sofa, eager to seize the

moment. If they both kept busy, the day would seem less long.

"If you can be ready to leave in the next half hour, I shall treat you at Gunter's Tea Shop. How does that sound?" she said.

The tentative smile which appeared on Patience's face was a great relief. She came to Alice's side and slipped a hand about her waist, dropping a kiss on her cheek. "Thank you, sister dearest. I can always count on you to help me out of an unhappy mood. Yes, we will go and spend the morning in town, and a flavored ice from Gunter's sounds perfect."

Small steps forward.

An hour later, Alice was standing at the counter of a small button seller in the Pantheon Bazaar on Oxford Street, silently congratulating herself on having eschewed the crush of Harding and Howell's for her and Patience's shopping trip. The bazaar was an interesting mix of shops and zoological gardens. One could buy all manner of items at the various stores, then go and see a real live monkey.

The only downside to the place was the loungers—small groups of well-dressed young men who hung around just to be seen. Every time they passed by any of the gentlemen who bore the slightest resemblance to Cuthbert Saint, Patience would let out a small sob.

Alice put her change and purchases into her reticule and turned to her sister. "Are you ready to go and get something to eat?"

Patience softly smiled. "Not quite. I would like a few minutes by myself."

A cold chill slid down Alice's back. Was Patience going to go somewhere and have another little cry all alone? She had appeared to be getting through the day without falling apart, but as she was beginning to discover for herself, broken hearts were unpredictable.

"I am fine. I just have some presents I wish to purchase

without you being with me. Even big sisters deserve surprises at Christmas," said Patience.

Alice softly chortled. She especially loved unwrapping gifts on Christmas Eve. "Alright. In the meantime, I shall go and rest my feet at the tea shop at the entrance to Marlborough Street. You can meet me there when you are done."

A cup of hot tea and a slice of buttered bun was top of Alice's list. That and a note to Harry. For while she had been doing her utmost to help Patience forget about Cuthbert Saint, there was nothing Alice could do to get Harry Steele out of her mind.

As soon as they were home, she would send word to him and try to meet. There was no point in putting off the worst if he wasn't interested in furthering their relationship.

But is it over between us? He looked hurt yesterday. Could it be that he might feel the same way I do?

Until Harry finally told her 'no,' there would always be a tiny flame of hope alight in her heart. A fire that only he could snuff out. Or set to a roaring blaze.

Chapter Seventeen

❦

Harry turned the note over and read it yet again.
Not a lot of sleep was had here last night on both our counts. Patience is coping as best as can be expected. The good news is that she wants to attend a ball tonight, so fingers crossed.

Final payment is due to you for the end of our contract. Please let me know if you wish the money sent. Or should I deliver it personally?

Alice.

He carefully folded Alice's letter and put it into his jacket pocket, then went back to staring out the drawing-room window. His gaze settled on the rain which had been falling constantly for the past half hour. There was something soothing about its steady rhythm.

It was the end of a long and, for Harry, reflective day. He drew little comfort from knowing that he had not been the only one to have endured a restless night.

From a safe distance, he had witnessed Cuthbert Saint get on board the coach bound for Harwich, only coming out from his hiding place after it had pulled out of the yard at the rear of the Spread Eagle Coaching Company. He and Stephen had then headed next door to the RR Coaching Company and polished off half a bottle of whisky in quiet celebration after he'd sent word to his associates to call off their Cuthbert watch.

The job was done. Patience North had been saved from an imprudent marriage, but even as the alcohol slipped down his throat, a sense of despondency had taken hold.

I almost wish Cuthbert hadn't taken the coins and left. Then I would have a good excuse to see Alice once more.

It was over between them before it had really begun. Her missive was polite, dare he say friendly, but all she really wanted to know was how he wished to receive his payment.

Did he want her to put some coins into a bag and send a footman over with it? Or perhaps a courier from the bank with a note. Both solutions would see money in his pocket and their connection at an end. Cold, clear, and impersonal.

His lack of sleep the previous night, had not just been due to the worry over what Alice had said, it was the fear that he had truly lost her. No other woman made him feel the way she did. Set his blood to near boiling point every time she was within arm's reach.

The memory of that night at the Temple of Diana, when she had finally shown her true self to him played over and over in Harry's mind. Her cry as she reached completion was a siren's call to him. He lusted after Alice, ached to once more explore her sweet body with his hands and lips. But it was more than just a deep seated sexual need. It went to his very soul; touched him deep on a primal level.

"Damn the money. I want her," he muttered.

Crossing to his desk, Harry took out a piece of paper and sat to pen his short reply.

I need to see you.

Harry

"If you are going to walk out of my life, I have to hear it from your own lips."

He folded the note and wrote Alice's name and address on

the front. If she and Patience were out this evening, then it would have to wait until morning.

Bang. Bang. Bang.

"What the devil?"

Someone was downstairs knocking loudly and insistently on the front door. Harry bolted from his chair and made for the stairs.

"I'm coming—just hold on!" he cried.

The banging continued on unabated as he crossed the tiled foyer and skidded to a halt at the front door.

"Alright, alright. Could you at least save the hinges?" he said, pulling the door open.

With hand raised ready to pound the timbers once more stood Alice. She was soaking wet, her clothes in a terrible state. Her long dark hair was plastered to her head.

"Oh, thank god you are home!" She pushed her way inside and slammed the door behind her. For a moment, she stood dripping water on the floor while she caught her breath. "Patience is gone," she whispered.

"What?"

"Cuthbert came back for her. They are going to elope."

Oh, bollocks. "But I saw him get on board the coach last night. How the hell did this happen?" he replied.

And you called off the watch dogs, so no one was following Patience. You dolt!

Alice threw up her hands. "Patience went for a walk this morning, and of course I didn't think anything of it. From what I can gather, Cuthbert must have tracked her down at that time, and convinced her to go to the party we were at tonight. She disappeared some thirty minutes ago, and then a footman eventually came and handed me her note."

Think. Think. What is to be done? Where could they be?

Harry clenched his fists, angry with himself for having underestimated Cuthbert. "I know this is a stupid question, but would you have any idea as to where they were headed?

The problem being that there are dozens of coaching companies in London; it would be nigh on impossible to catch them if we don't know their destination," he replied.

Alice sighed. "You said that Cuthbert was on the run from Scotland. Which means they might not head north. If they don't, they will need a marriage license in England. If they want to get an ordinary license, they are going to have to hide out somewhere until they can find a minister. So, no, I have absolutely no idea where they could be headed."

The desperation in her voice was heartbreaking.

Harry took a step back and sought to clear his mind. There was a piece of the puzzle missing. "The Grand Hotel. That is our best chance," he said.

"Why?"

"When Stephen took Cuthbert last night, they went directly to the coaching company. I can only hope that our friend has gone back to the hotel to retrieve his things. If not, we may have a real problem on our hands."

He was grasping at straws, but it was the only thing that made sense in the moment. And it was all he had. "Wait here; I'll get my pistol. This blackguard clearly only understands violence."

"What about your other friends, could they assist?" she replied.

Harry was already halfway up the stairs. There wasn't time to send word to the other members of the RR Coaching Company. If they didn't intercept Cuthbert and Patience at the Grand Hotel, they would never be able to stop them fleeing London.

"Too late!" he cried.

He was back in under a minute, more than a little grateful that Stephen had had the good sense to always have a cleaned and loaded pistol on the top of the dresser in his room.

"Tell me you made the carriage wait for you when you got here?" he said.

"Yes, of course."

Grosvenor Street to Covent Gardens was a journey of little over a mile, but every minute Harry and Alice spent in the carriage was time when he worried that they may arrive at the Grand Hotel just a minute too late.

As the hack slowed and turned into the rear mews, Harry flung the door open and jumped out. The momentum set him at a run from the time he hit the ground.

Out of the corner of his eye, he caught sight of a footman carrying a bag down the stairs, heading for a nearby carriage. He didn't have time to consider whether it was Cuthbert's bag or not.

"Stop!" he bellowed.

The footman reared back in surprise at the sight of Harry running full pelt at him while brandishing a pistol.

The footman dropped the bag. "Please. Please don't shoot me. I only work here."

The carriage door opened, and Cuthbert Saint stepped out.

"I think I am the man you are looking for, Lord Steele," he said.

He turned and helped Patience North down from the carriage. At the same time, Alice appeared at Harry's side.

"Oh, thank God we found you. I would never have forgiven myself if we didn't," she said.

The expression on Patience's face was less favorable. She glared at her sister. "I knew you were behind all this; you couldn't let me be happy. Are you so jealous that you would keep me from my true love?"

Harry shot a look in the direction of the hotel footman; his eyes were wide with interest. He couldn't blame the man. It wasn't every day that a domestic drama was played out in the rear mews of a posh London hotel.

"Do you think we could have a few minutes privacy somewhere inside?" asked Harry.

Cuthbert frowned, but to Harry's relief, Patience finally lived up to her name. "Alright. Let's go and talk. If anything, it will give me the opportunity to say a proper goodbye to my sister."

The four of them followed the footman back inside and were shown into a downstairs sitting room. There was a twin pair of soft, leather couches, but no one took a seat.

Harry closed and locked the door before leaning back on it. No one would be leaving the room without his say so. The pistol remained pointed at Cuthbert.

He was about to say something when Alice suddenly rounded on her sister and let fly. "Are you out of your mind, Patience? That man is nothing more than a cold, heartless blackguard who only wants to wed you for money. I was trying to protect you from making a momentous mistake. Instead of attacking me, you should be saying thank you."

Patience came and stood by Cuthbert's side, slipping her hand into his arm.

Shit. This is not good. He has her on his side.

The fact that they were in a hotel meant the chances of Harry being able to shoot Cuthbert and get away with it were nil. And without the assistance of his fellow rogues, he wouldn't even be able to stage a decent kidnapping. Damn.

Time to see who will blink first.

He took a chance and cocked the pistol, aiming it at Cuthbert's heart.

"Cuthbert Saint, or should I say Cuthbert Leigh, it is time you told Miss Patience North the truth. I want to hear your full confession here and now or I shall pull the trigger."

Patience nodded at Cuthbert. "Go on. Tell them everything."

The look which passed between the couple tore the last vestiges of hope from Harry. They were in love, and unless he was prepared to commit murder, there wasn't a damn thing he could do to keep them apart.

Cuthbert faced Alice. "Yes, I came to London seeking a wife with means. I chose your sister because she was kind enough to speak to me at a party. Once I understood who she was and the depth of your father's pockets, I decided to do all I could to woo and convince her to elope with me."

Alice put her hands together, prayerlike, and with tear-filled eyes turned to her sister. "See? He is a scoundrel. Now can we please go home and try to forget this ever happened? I won't even mention it to Mama and Papa."

"Alice, let him finish," said Patience.

Cuthbert gave a nod of appreciation. "I made every effort to get to know Patience, and the more time I spent with her, the more certain I became that I loved her. Miss Alice, it didn't take much for me to see that you were against us being together. I had hoped that in time you might come to view me in a different light, but then things started happening over the past few days and I realized you would never consider me good enough."

Harry frowned. He didn't like the way this conversation was headed.

"You mean, I employed someone to investigate and unmask you? Yes, I did. And I would do it again. Anything to stop my sister from throwing her life away," said Alice.

Patience let go of Cuthbert's arm and crossed the floor to Alice. She wore a gentle, determined smile on her face.

At least she is not angry.

"I know what I am doing, Alice. Cuthbert has told me everything. From what he did in Scotland, to the secret life he has been living here in London. He was waiting for me on the corner when I went for my walk this morning." Her gaze now shifted to Harry. "He even told me about the man who stole him off the street and forced him into a coach bound for the coast last night."

An awkward silence descended on the room. No one

seemed willing to speak, everyone silently aware that any further revelations might well shatter the fragile mood.

Cuthbert moved slowly toward Alice; his gaze still locked on the pistol. Patience slipped her hands into his.

"Your sister knows everything. And I am also aware of the financial arrangements which come with marrying one of you," he said.

Financial arrangements? What?

Alice huffed. "I don't give a damn. You are a liar and a thief—that's enough for me to know my sister should never marry you. Criminals don't belong in my family."

Her words went straight to Harry's heart like a sharp dagger. If Alice couldn't find a way to ever accept Cuthbert marrying Patience, he had no chance.

If only my wickedness began and ended with a few stolen trinkets.

"I'm sorry, Alice, but you don't get to decide this matter. When we were out this morning and you thought I was Christmas gift shopping, I was actually at the pawnbroker's buying back all the items which Cuthbert had sold to them. They are already on the mail coach to Scotland, returning to their rightful owner," said Patience.

For the second time in as many minutes, Harry found himself stunned. He was still reeling over Alice's declaration, but hearing that Cuthbert and Patience were set on restitution had him lowering his pistol and uncocking it. If anyone could understand the reasons for a man seeking a second chance in life it was Harry.

"What are you doing? The man is a villain!" exclaimed Alice.

"No. He is someone who made a grave error of judgement. We have all done that at some point in our lives. Even you, Alice," replied Harry.

She backed away from them all, creating a distance that spoke volumes for what she clearly thought of his words.

Alice slowly shook her head. "I can't believe this is happening. Harry, I paid you to break them apart, not take his side."

"Miss Alice. I have never done an evil thing before in my life. Taking those things was a moment of recklessness on my part. I saw the life that being in service was set for me to my dying days. Working all hours for a pittance and never a kind word. I am not trying to justify what I did—simply explain it. If I had my time again, I would have just walked away," said Cuthbert.

"And what about trying to seduce my sister?" replied Alice.

Cuthbert shook his head. "I fell in love with Patience the first time I met her. I just didn't know how I could find a way to be honest and still win her heart. In the end, I decided that the truth was all I could offer."

Patience lifted his hand to her lips and brushed a kiss on it. "You are a good man, Cuthbert; you just lost your way. I love you."

Despite what Alice wanted, there was nothing either of them could do. Patience was an adult, and if she was set on marrying Cuthbert, only publicly denouncing him would stop her from doing so. No matter what she might think of him, Harry couldn't stand idly by and let Alice destroy Cuthbert.

"May I suggest something?" he said.

He did his best to ignore the hopeful gaze Alice sent his way. If she was looking for him to be her savior, she was going to be disappointed.

"Once Mister and Mrs. North return to England, Cuthbert Saint shall make his introductions. Cuthbert Leigh will, of course, have to stay dead, but I don't see any of us having a problem with that. A proper courtship can then take place. That plan will depend on the four of us agreeing never to tell about the items which Cuthbert took and for his past to remain permanently hidden," said Harry.

"And I can give Cuthbert enough money to be able to live on in the meantime," added Patience.

Alice threw up her hands. "Utter madness." And with that, she headed for the door.

When she got to Harry, she fixed him with a hard, hateful look. "Get out of my way. And if I ever see you again, I will have you clasped in irons."

Chapter Eighteen

❦

Alice went home, found the key to her father's study, and helped herself to a full bottle of brandy from the sideboard. She still wasn't certain whether she particularly liked the drink or not, but after the events of the day, strong alcohol was well in order.

And none of that just a sniff in the bottom of the glass either.

She was sitting feet-up on the occasional table in the family sitting room, well into her second generous drink when Patience finally made it home.

Patience dropped onto the sofa next to her with a tired sigh. "When did you start getting a taste for brandy?"

Alice ignored her sister, making a great study of the foul liquid in her glass. The drink Harry had given her at the Temple of Diana should have been enough to inform her that she was not a brandy drinker.

"Alice?"

"I think we have said all we need to tonight. You have made your position clear and my opinion doesn't count," she replied.

Patience rose from the sofa and returned momentarily

with her own glass. She poured herself a generous serve then resumed her seat. The brandy went to her lips.

"Oh, that's awful. How can you drink that stuff?" she exclaimed.

Alice snorted. "I don't know, but after this evening's events, I decided I needed something strong."

Patience set her glass on the table, and Alice followed suit. Her sister moved along the sofa and gently took hold of her hand. Alice couldn't find it in herself to pull away. She was heartsore not just over Cuthbert and Patience, but also Harry.

He had betrayed her. At the moment she needed him to be strong and stand his ground, he had caved.

"You love Lord Harry Steele, don't you?"

She dropped her head. If only it wasn't so obvious to the rest of the world that she had fallen for the rogue. "No. He is just as big a blackguard as Cuthbert. I could never love a man such as that. It's impossible."

If only my heart believed that to be true. It would be so much easier.

"You are not as good a liar as you think, Alice. I knew you were up to something the day I saw you talking to Lord Harry Steele. He is not the sort of man you in particular would give the time of day to unless there was a reason. You might think you were watching me make a fool of myself over Cuthbert, but I have seen the hungry looks you give to Harry. Deny it all you wish; it's as plain as day that you love him."

This wasn't how it was meant to transpire. Harry was to warn Cuthbert away, rescue Patience from herself, and then be gone from her life.

But from that first night at Viscount Ashton's ball, he had slowly worked his way into her heart. Stolen kiss by stolen kiss, he had claimed her. She had given him more than just money, he owned her soul.

That night at the club had cast aside any lingering doubts

she may have had about the two of them. He had told her she was living in a cage, and the moment she came under his hand, Harry had set her free.

"What are you afraid of?" asked Patience.

Nothing. Everything. The truth.

If the Harry that everyone thought they knew was a ruse, and that night he had given her a glimpse of his real world, what else lay beyond? She would give anything to spend the rest of her life exploring it with him.

She met her sister's gaze. Cuthbert had confessed all to Patience and their love had survived. Could she do the same with Harry? "I am afraid that if I ask Lord Harry Steele to tell me the truth of who he is and the life he leads, that no matter how shocking it is, I will still be in love with him."

An arm came around her shoulder and she lay her head against Patience. The day had been long, and exhaustion threatened to overtake her.

"I can tell you from my own experience, that your heart decides who you love. Sense and rational thought don't always come into it. I tried not to fall for Cuthbert; he was too good to be true. But he and I were always meant to be."

As Alice's eyes drifted closed, Harry's words from that night at the Temple of Diana slipped back into her mind. *"Break free of that cage and embrace who you are."*

She was done with fighting her destiny. Tomorrow, she would confront Harry and demand he release her from all the lies and pain that stood between them.

Only then could she truly be free of her gilded cage. Only then could there be any possible hope for them.

Chapter Nineteen

"I am going to hold you to the promise that you and Cuthbert won't elope while I am gone."

Patience rolled her eyes. "We are not going anywhere until after the wedding. And we won't be getting married before Mama and Papa return home. I was never that keen on eloping anyway."

Alice glanced behind her sister's back, making sure she wasn't crossing her fingers as she spoke. She was still finding it difficult to accept that Patience and Cuthbert would soon be married; it would take time for her to learn to trust her future brother-in-law.

The truce between the two North sisters was still holding. Their friendship and sisterly affection might well be bruised but loyalty had finally won out.

As she and Patience stood in the grand entrance to their family home, Alice pondered whether it was wise for her to go and see Harry. She had said some truly awful things to him at the hotel. Her last words to him having been spoken in anger and pain. If he refused to see her, she could hardly blame him.

"Will you please get in the carriage and go and do something about Harry Steele?" urged Patience.

Alice gratefully accepted her sister's reassuring hug.

I have to do this, though I fear what sort of welcome I may receive. Take a chance. Apologize. What is the worst that could happen?

The worst could be that her stubborn nature had already destroyed any chance she might have with the man her heart had decided was her destiny.

Alice closed the clasp of her cloak and, after accepting another hug from Patience, headed out to the rear mews and the North family carriage.

She gave the footman a brief "Thank you," and stepped aboard.

"Good morning. I was beginning to wonder if you were ever going to leave."

Her mouth opened on a small 'O' as she took in the sight of Harry Steele lazing in the far corner. She dropped onto the opposite bench just as the door was closed.

Harry rapped on the roof and the carriage gave a lurch as the horses pulled up the slack.

Alice turned and caught a glimpse of Patience standing on the steps of the house, waving them goodbye. A huge, knowing grin sat on her lips.

"Your sister is far more cunning than I gave her credit for," he said.

"I don't understand," replied Alice.

Harry shuffled over and came to sit by her side. Tears pricked in her eyes at the sight of him—at the hopeful smile he wore.

"Patience sent a note early this morning, said the two of you had reached some sort of détente when it came to hostilities over Cuthbert. That when your parents return to England you will support her and Cuthbert's decision to marry. She also said you were possibly having second thoughts over never wanting to see me again," he said.

Alice slowly shook her head. "I'm still at sixes and sevens over you. I just know that the only way I am going to find any sort of resolution is for us to sit and talk. And when I say talk, I mean an open discussion about everything, including your other life."

"Good. Then that is what we shall do," he replied.

The carriage travelled on out of Mortimer Street, and it was only when it turned into Oxford Street that she finally thought to ask him where they were going.

"This isn't the way to your home," she said.

"No. Stephen is hosting one of his own client's this morning, so I thought it best if we went elsewhere. Neutral ground, for want of a better term," he replied.

She scowled at him. He had better not be taking her to the bloody Temple of Diana.

Then again. Remember what happened last time you went there?

He raised an eyebrow and she silently cursed him.

You always know exactly what I am thinking. Such a rogue. And so damn alluring.

"We are going to the Grand Hotel. After last night, I owe the footman a coin or two. And since Cuthbert has checked out and gone to stay with a friend of mine, we know they have a vacancy."

Alice gasped. He patted her on the arm. "Relax, we are not staying in his old room. That would be even too creepy for me."

"I don't recall agreeing to stay in a hotel room with you. What if we are seen arriving? How am I going to explain that to my parents?" she replied.

There was a raft of things that the North siblings, including the elusive Finn, were going to have to tell Mister and Mrs. North once they returned home. She could only pray that news of Patience and Cuthbert's romance silenced much of the other items which were on the list for discussion.

Their gazes met. The grin had gone from Harry's face. In its place was a look of heartbreaking sincerity. He leaned in and kissed her softly on the lips.

"We will arrive by the servants' entrance. I want you to know that if you don't like what you hear from me, you can leave the hotel with your reputation still intact," he said.

"Thank you."

If this all ended in tears, her good name might be the only thing which Alice could salvage from today.

Chapter Twenty

⚜

At the hotel, Harry took Alice by the hand and led her quickly up a set of stairs at the back. Coming through a doorway on the second floor, they stepped out into a plushy carpeted hallway. Harry unlocked a nearby door and ushered her through it.

Alice's gaze swept the room and she turned to him. "Oh, this is rather lovely."

The suite Harry had booked for them was the most expensive one the Grand Hotel could offer. The arrival of his smuggler companion, Gus Jones, late the previous night, pockets laden with coins, meant Harry was fortunately flush with funds.

Their room was sumptuously decorated. Dark blue curtains trimmed with gold tassels were drawn closed over the windows. The coverlet of the enormous bed was similarly decorated in blue and gold stripes. The Prince of Wales could easily stay here and feel right at home.

"Here. Let me help you with your cloak," he offered.

She hesitated for a moment, only seeming to finally relax when he removed his own coat and lay it over a high-backed chair. He returned to her side, letting out a small sigh of relief when Alice set her fingers to the buttons and unclasped the cloak.

Harry took it and Alice's reticule, and set them on the table which sat between the two windows.

"Would you like a glass of champagne?" he said.

"I would prefer it if we talked first. Clear head and all," she replied.

It was understandable, and as much as he could kill a glass of something strong right now, Harry held back.

"Where would you like to sit?" he asked.

Alice's gaze fell on the sensible table and chairs, but her feet moved her in the direction of a sofa, which sat across the end of the bed.

Thank god. The last thing I want to do is to be trying to talk to her across a table.

Harry joined Alice on the sofa, sitting at a polite distance. Much as he ached to hold her in his arms and kiss her, this was one conversation which he dared not muddy with physicality.

She turned to him and nodded. "There are a thousand questions rolling around in my mind. The most important being, do you want a future with me?"

"Yes," he answered without hesitation.

"Alright, then I am ready to hear what you have to say about your life, and what I could be letting myself in for if we did agree to bind our lives together," she replied.

Harry raked his fingers through his hair. Last night, he had rehearsed this speech, but now in the cold light of day and in front of Alice, it wasn't so easy to deliver.

"Long story short. As you can probably guess, I am not the sort of man designed to take to the career path that most other younger sons do. The military, the priesthood, and going off to a far-flung colony were never on my list. A year ago, my father and I argued over this, and he cut me off without a penny."

It wasn't anything Alice hadn't heard before, but nerves had Harry wanting to firstly cover familiar ground.

"Go on."

"Some friends of mine have also faced similar life choices and decided that they had skill sets more suited to . . . hmm." Thinking and practicing the words were not the same as actually saying them.

This is the woman I love, and I could be about to lose her.

Harry swallowed a large lump of fear.

A warm hand settled on his thigh. Alice nodded, silently encouraging him to continue.

"We set up an enterprise called the RR Coaching Company. It's a bit of a spin on an old jest about us being rogues of the road. Officially, it is supposed to be a coaching business out of premises in Gracechurch Street. But in reality, it is a front for the rest of our not-so-scrupulous dealings."

"But you met with me at your home," she replied.

"I can meet with clients in my private residence because this rogue-for-hire endeavor is legitimate work. The rest of what we get up to has to remain hidden."

Beside him, Alice sighed, and Harry's heart sank. He had come this far. There was no point in keeping the rest of the details of his secret life from her. Alice deserved to know everything.

"What you are saying then is that you operate in what my father would call grey areas?" she asked.

If only it were that simple. While it was tempting to say yes and let Alice think that what he and the rest of the members of the RR Coaching Company did was a small step the other side of the law, Harry was determined not to begin or see the end of their relationship on a lie. "There are some things we are involved in which couldn't remotely be classed as grey. There is nothing legal whatsoever in smuggled and stolen goods. Sir Stephen Moore and I have dabbled in blackmail, threats, and the odd kidnapping."

Alice got to her feet. She stood for a time with her back to him, head bowed.

Harry then continued. "Alice I . . ."

She held up a hand, and Harry stopped talking. He nodded. She had obviously heard enough.

Well, at least it is out in the open. She knows the sort of man I am. I am a rogue.

With uncertain steps, Alice made her way toward the table where Harry had put her cloak and reticule. She was leaving. Of course, she was. If Alice couldn't find it in her heart to accept Cuthbert Saint and his failings, how had he ever thought she could see her way to loving him?

"You do realize that you will never be able to tell my parents any of this if we marry. Cuthbert's secret is bad enough, but this is far worse," she said.

You could have knocked Harry over with a feather. Alice was still talking as if they had a future. He shrugged off his shock and got to his feet, racing to her side.

He held a tentative hand out to her. "No one in any of our families are aware of what we do. The eventual hope is that the RR Coaching Company will become a proper coaching business and we can move away from some of the less salubrious sides of the business. The last thing I want is for any of us to face the law and hang for our crimes."

Alice stared at the floor for the longest time—so long that Harry began to worry that he had just shot himself in the foot by mentioning the death sentence. When she met his gaze, tears shone in her eyes.

He couldn't hold himself back—he reached for Alice and drew her gently into his arms. A kiss on her forehead was the most he dared risk.

"Thank you for finally telling me the truth of things. I had hoped that drawing pistols on people might be the extent of it, but even I didn't believe that to be more than a fanciful wish," she replied.

"If it is of any comfort, I can assure you that we are good at what we do and also covering our tracks. George's father is a judge, and none of us want to ever be brought before him," he said.

Alice pulled out of his embrace, sniffing back her tears. "I'll have that champagne now please, Harry."

But champagne is for happiness, for rejoicing.

He wanted nothing more than to marry this girl. To claim her and be the best husband she could ever wish to have. That would be the greatest cause for celebration.

Seize the moment and never let go.

He began to dip down on his knee in readiness to propose to her, but Alice shook her head. "Not until after you have heard the terms of my marriage settlement. You may not wish to make me your wife after I tell you what they are."

"If you will take me as I am, I don't care what draconian clauses your father has welded into your dowries. My desire to be with you has never been about money."

Chapter Twenty-One

Harry wasn't the only one in possession of a surprise. Alice had kept the details of her dowry a closely guarded secret.

While Harry opened the bottle of champagne and poured them both a glass, Alice got the words of the settlement clear in her mind. "Papa has written ironclad marriage contracts for both Patience and me. If we tell him that we don't want our husbands to receive funds, you get nothing. No money is settled immediately upon marriage."

Harry chuckled. "I bet that came as a nasty shock to Cuthbert."

"Actually, it was the final thing that convinced me he really does love my sister. He can neither kiss nor kick her dowry out of her. The lifestyle he will be granted in the years to come is very much dependent on her goodwill." She accepted the glass of champagne he offered her and took a sip.

"But if that is the case, then why were you so set against the marriage? Cuthbert cannot get his hands on a vast fortune. I don't understand," he replied.

"Because as you yourself said, it was never about the

money. I only ever wanted to save Patience from marrying a man who didn't love her. It's not as if either of us wander around society informing potential husbands that they are not about to land a large sack of money on their wedding day. Last night, Patience told me that Cuthbert Saint wasn't aware of the terms of the marriage settlements until yesterday morning."

"And yet he still wanted to marry her."

"Yes. Love will do that to a man, or so I've been told."

Harry held his glass up. "A toast to you, Alice North. I have never met anyone like you before. You challenge everything I thought I had clear in my mind. Not that that is always a good thing, but I still love you for it."

You love me. Oh, Harry.

The tears came back full force this time. "You love me?" she whispered.

"Yes. I would never have taken you to the Temple of Diana if I didn't think you and I belonged together. Though I must confess that at the time, I wasn't sure if you felt something strongly for me, so I held back. Alice, you have made me share things about myself with you that I haven't done with anyone else."

Harry slipped a hand around her waist and planted a kiss on her lips. "It took every ounce of my self-control not to make you mine that night. You set things off in me that no other woman ever has; a deep burning desire for you flamed the moment we met. But I was determined that you would know the best and the worst about me before I put you in a position where marriage was the inevitable outcome of our relationship."

Alice wiped at her tears. She had thought his refusal to make love to her that night was his way of rejecting her. That he hadn't seen her as a potential wife.

"I would have given myself to you that night, and I wouldn't have regretted it. I love you, Harry Steele. I love your madness, your outrageous dress sense, even your cute little piglet."

He raised both eyebrows at those words. "And my wicked ways?"

She pursed her lips. There could never be a point where she could see herself being comfortable with the dangerous and illegal things that he and his friends did. "Only if you promise that in the years to come, you will do everything to move the RR Coaching Company to a respectable footing. I know you have powerful family and friends, but there may come a time when they cannot protect you."

"I promise. In return, I want your answer to my question." Harry went down on bended knee.

This time, Alice didn't stop him. The choice now lay with her. Was she prepared to set aside her concerns, and consider a future with this rogue, relying on his promise that one day they would be free of danger?

Her heart whispered its answer. The one she would never be able to deny.

Yes.

"Alice North, I love you. I want to spend the rest of my life with you. And I want to spend as much of that time as possible in respectable, wedded bliss. Will you marry me?"

There were times they had both pushed things to their limit. But if this was the life they could have as husband and wife, one where they were equals and striving forward together, Alice wanted it.

It was such a relief that all the doubts and questions which had been preying on her mind were now out in the open. The road ahead would not be easy. Until the day Harry told her he was no longer involved in shady dealings, Alice would always worry. But she had made up her mind and would now stand beside him, helping him to create a better life.

"Yes."

Harry got to his feet, and Alice stepped into his embrace,

accepting his tender kisses with a grateful smile. A smile which turned into a longing sigh as his lips found their way to the side of her neck. He gently nipped, and heat pooled in her loins.

Memories of that night at the club came flooding back into her mind. No matter how long she lived, Alice would never forget that moment when Harry had brought her to climax as she lay on the floor.

Soon enough, she would ask Harry to take her back to the Temple of Diana, for him to show her more of that side of herself. But here and now, she was going to seize the moment.

They were alone in a luxury hotel suite. They were engaged. There was nothing and no one to stop them indulging in whatever they wished.

"Harry?" she whispered.

"Hmm." His lips were in the crook of her neck, his hot breath sending shock waves of desire through her body.

She lifted a hand and ran her fingers through his hair, ruffling it gently when she reached the long wayward mop on top. Was there ever a sexier hairstyle for a man? She was certain there was not. "You could have had this discussion with me at my home, so I am assuming you brought me here because you had a plan which involved more than talking."

You had better have plans or I am going to have to take a stand for both of us.

His body shook as a chuckle rumbled through him. Her whole core clenched at the sound. What his laugh did to her was beyond anything she had ever imagined humor could do.

Harry lifted his head and met her gaze. "Actually, I hadn't got much further than rehearsing what I was going to say. Trust me though, I am a man used to making things up on the fly. Improvisation is one of my strong suits, so the day will not be wasted."

Alice grinned at him. Harry, the gorgeously, sexy man was

back, and she wanted him. Wanted to share her all with him today.

His fingers toyed with the opening of her gown. Alice lay her hand over his and whispered, "I want to keep these undergarments; they are some of my favorites. So, please don't go getting any ideas about tearing them to pieces."

Harry flashed his stunning green eyes at her. Alice shook her head. If she succumbed every time, he chose to use his sexual weapons on her, she would never win a battle.

"Harry Steele, you are not allowed to play unfairly when it comes to the bedroom. If you do, punishment shall follow."

Harry groaned. "Oh, Alice, you have no idea what that does to me. If you are going to be strict, I promise I will misbehave all the damn time."

She swiped playfully at him. "Naughty boy."

As the topmost button on the front of her gown opened, Harry leaned in and kissed her. The next button saw another kiss. And so, it went on. By the time he had worked his way down the line of the dozen small fastenings, they were both breathing heavily. Harry then made fast work of Alice's stays before discarding them and her gown.

Now, she was determined that Harry would also know pleasure. They were in this together, and she wanted him to experience all that she felt for him.

She brushed her hand over the placket of his trousers and Harry groaned once more. Unlike last time, he didn't push her away.

What a pity you are not wearing a toga. I could take you in hand so much faster.

"Promise me that you will tell me how you like to be touched. How I can give you the pleasure you need. Don't be afraid that I will hold back. I want us to know everything about the other, even our darkest desires," she said.

He took a hold of her breast, brushing his fingers back and forth over her peaked nipple. The sensation even through the thin fabric of her chemise sent heat pooling in her loins. Her body ached for him to show her the heady heights of sex once more.

"We will take things slowly. There is far more enjoyment in a slow, sensual dance than a fast waltz. Today, I want to know you as my woman, for our bodies to reach climax together."

Alice swallowed deeply. She wanted this, trusted Harry to show her the way. He took her lips in another long, soft kiss.

When he released her, Harry held her gaze. "Do you remember the night at the club, when I asked for your permission? We are going to do that again. I want you to always feel that you are in control of what is happening to your body, of your sexual release."

Her answer to each and every one of his requests was going to be yes.

"Harry, make love to me," she replied.

He nodded. His jacket and cravat were quickly dealt with, his boots toed off and flung into a corner.

When they came together once more, Harry was clad only in his shirt and trousers, the placket of which was partly undone. Alice stared longingly at the bulge which pressed against the remaining fastenings.

She held a hand to her chemise and shyly smiled at him. "Remember, no ripping."

Harry placed his hands either side of her body, then slowly began to bunch the fabric up in his hands. Inch by inch, the chemise lifted.

Cool air kissed her calves, then her thighs. When the hem of the garment barely covered her hips, he stopped.

"May I?" he asked.

"Yes."

There was a whoosh of fabric, her vision momentarily covered, and then Alice was free of her chemise. She stood only in her stockings and slippers. The shoes went the same way as Harry's, into the corner.

Alice slipped a hand down and covered her sex, earning herself a disapproving shake of the head from Harry.

She bent to remove her stockings.

"No, they stay on," he said.

She scowled; why would he want her to keep her stockings on?

"You have no idea of the nights I have lain awake and thought of you naked except for your stockings. Of how many times I taken myself in hand and stroked my length just thinking how amazing it would feel to be deep inside you with your stocking-clad legs wrapped around me."

"I see. So, the stockings stay, but the rest of me is naked?" she replied.

He moved her hand away from where it covered her sex.

"Never be ashamed of your body, my love, especially not in front of me. I intend that you will spend a great deal of time naked, so you may as well get used to it," he said.

She raised an eyebrow at his remark. "Breakfast naked? Doing the household accounts naked? What about when we fight?"

Harry stepped forward and gently placed his hands on her hips. "I look forward to listening to you yell at me when you are naked. I can just picture how your breasts will bounce up and down the more riled you get. Fighting then fucking will be the order of our marriage. I shall demand it."

She pretended to be shocked by his rough language, but having heard it from her brother enough times, Alice couldn't muster the right expression. Instead she simply laughed.

He pulled her against him, his hard erection pushing against her stomach. Emboldened by their honest conversation, Alice dropped her hand to the last button on his trousers and flicked it open. Harry's cock leapt free and into her hand. She squeezed gently, then began to stroke him.

He let her toy with him for a time, his breathing slowly growing more ragged by the second. Resting his hand on hers, he stilled her movement.

"Enough, woman. Time for you to be ravished." After scooping her up in his arms, Harry marched over to the bed and promptly tossed her onto it. His shirt and trousers disappeared in an instant and a naked Harry climbed on, rising over Alice.

He stilled, staring deep into her eyes. "Where to begin? It's like being given a huge menu and not knowing which dish you want to start with."

She grinned up at him. "We do have all day, so we could feast for quite some time."

His gaze shifted to her breasts and he gave an appreciative hum. "I started with those last time, so I think I might leave them to the next course."

Alice's hips bucked as Harry traced a finger down her stomach and brushed over the outer folds of her sex. Her body thrummed with desire. He was barely touching her, but the memory of his fingers and what he could do with them had her panting. "Yes. Yes. Anything," she whispered.

One, two fingers dipped into her wet heat. She was not the least surprised that his strokes were so easily deep and long, she had been ripe and ready for him from the moment he had first kissed her. Alice was hungry for his touch.

Pleasure coursed through her body as he slowly thrust his fingers in and out. His thumb rolled exquisite circles around her sensitive bud and she groaned.

I will never be able to get enough of this, of what he does to me.

Harry shifted further down the bed. Alice's back arched off the mattress as his hot mouth and tongue began to feast on the soft flesh of her sex. Her fingers clutched at the bedclothes, grabbing and holding them in tight fistfuls.

"Oh my god, Harry," she whimpered.

Her climax was near; it took all her strength not to beg

him to finish her off. She was desperate to come, but not this way.

"Tell me what you want," he said.

"I want you inside me. I don't care what else we do this afternoon. I just want this first time, and now," she whispered.

He positioned himself between her legs, his cock large and hard in his hand. She flinched for a moment as he pressed himself inside. There was a momentary sting and then it was gone.

Harry stilled. "When you are ready, let me know." He traced his thumb around and over her sensitive nib, and Alice gripped his arms.

She let out a shuddering breath. "Yes. Please. I want this."

He pushed all the way in, and she moaned. "Oh, Harry, that is so good. Please, I need more."

A steady rhythm of deep thrusts and withdrawal began. She had never imagined it could be this way with a man. That her first time would be so incredible, the groans of pleasure which came from Harry making the encounter all that more glorious.

The bed rocked with his every move. Alice closed her eyes and gave herself up to him. Let Harry take control of her body and her ever-growing hunger.

Her need built to fever-pitch. She was so close to release, but it was just out of reach. In a sudden movement, Harry pulled back, and taking one of her breasts into his mouth, sucked hard. It was all it took to push her over the edge.

"Harry, oh!"

Alice's world exploded.

The orgasm he had given her at the club was nothing compared to this mind-altering climax. Pleasure tore through her like lightening. On and on it rolled.

"Wrap your legs around me. Take me deeper," he commanded.

She lifted her stockinged legs and did as he asked. Harry buried his face in the crook of her neck as he pounded his cock deeper, harder and faster with every stroke. His fingers gripped to the side of her hips, his breath coming shorter every second.

And then he let out a guttural groan and slammed into her one last time. They collapsed into each other's arms, panting for air. Hot, sweat-slicked bodies held tight to each other.

When Harry finally rolled off Alice, he pulled her to him. "I love you," he whispered.

"I love you too."

※

In the late evening, Harry eventually took Alice home. They had shared a long afternoon of making love and exploring one another's bodies. He had lost count of the times he had brought her to climax, but the memory of hearing her cry his name when she was on the verge of release would forever remain in his heart.

The carriage slowed to a stop in the mews at the rear of the North family home, and Harry helped Alice down. They walked toward the house, hand in hand.

As they passed the main entrance to the stables, Alice paused mid-stride, before stumbling to a halt. She pointed to a large travel coach which had not been in the yard when Harry had arrived earlier in the day.

"Oh, thank heavens," she exclaimed.

"What?"

She turned to him, and cupping his face in her hands, gifted him with a hundred kisses. She then drew back, smiling. "That's the North family travel coach. My parents have come home early from their trip."

Chapter Twenty-Two

❦

The following afternoon, Harry walked the short distance from his house in Grosvenor Street to Redditch House. It was only a matter of a hundred yards or so to his family home in Upper Grosvenor Street, but at times over the past year, it had felt like an ocean separated them.

He got a welcoming smile from the head butler as he stepped in the front door of the early Georgian mansion. The house took up a great deal of the block with its imposing Portland columns; the dukes of Redditch were never ones to hold back on showing their wealth.

Upstairs, Harry waited outside his father's study. For the first time in his life, he wasn't nervous about seeing Lord Steele. The man had already cut him off and thrown him out of the house. There was nothing left for his father to hold over his head.

"Your grace, your son is here to see you."

The sound of a throat being cleared, and gruff mumbling drifted out to where Harry stood.

"Which one? I have four of the beggars," replied Lord Steele.

"My apologies. Lord Harry Steele."

Silence followed, and Harry could just imagine what foul curses would be running through his father's mind at the mere mention of his name.

Nice to see you too, Papa.

"Alright, show him in."

He quickly checked his jacket and cravat in the hall mirror, making sure they were all in order. Taking a deep breath, he straightened his back and strode into the Duke of Redditch's study.

His gaze took in the all too familiar room. Books, piles of papers, and the ever-present cigar hanging out of his father's mouth greeted him.

Harry caught the scent of burning tobacco and smiled. "Port-tipped. I thought you had given up on those."

Lord Steele raised his eyes from where they had been staring at a ledger and fixed his gaze on Harry. "A year, and that is all you have to say to me?"

"I thought I would go with something innocuous to begin with, recalling that the last time we spoke you were raining down hellfire and brimstone on me," replied Harry.

His father rose from his desk, setting his cigar on an ashtray where it continued to send out a small, thin plume of smoke. "And as I recall, you were telling me to 'go to the blasted devil,' so I think we might call that even."

Harry grinned at the memory. At the time, there had been nothing amusing about it, but over the past eleven and a bit months, he had made his peace with it—mostly.

He took a moment to study his father; little had changed about his features during the period of their estrangement. The man had barely aged a day. There was comfort in seeing that the old bastard was still fighting fit. They might not currently see eye to eye, but he could confess to having a soft spot somewhere in his heart for his father.

Lord Steele came around to the front of his desk and gave Harry a slow looking over.

I dressed in my best courting clothes today. He can't possibly have any cause to find fault with my attire.

"Are you well, boy?" he asked.

Harry chuckled. He was twenty-six years old, and had long ago stopped being a lad, yet his father still referred to him as if he was a child.

"Yes, Father, I am in excellent health," he replied.

A half sniff and a nod were his father's reply. He pointed toward the nearby whisky-laden sideboard. "Fancy a drink?"

There was meaning behind those words. Lord Steele's offer wasn't so much one of being a convivial host, but rather subtly enquiring as to whether he would need a stiff drink, or two once Harry revealed the purpose for his visit.

"Thank you, no. I have had a morning of champagne, and that was plenty enough."

"Champagne? You are a strange one, Harry Steele. If I wasn't sure that your mother has always been true to me, I would think you might be someone else's by-blow," replied the duke.

At times, Harry suspected it might have been easier for his father to deal with him if had thought he might not be his son. The nobility was not known for keeping to the marital bed, but in his parents' case, they had. A rare love which had blossomed from an arranged marriage had seen the duke and duchess happily wed for almost forty years.

"I was celebrating with my future bride and her family; that was the reason for the champagne. I am getting married, Father," said Harry.

Genuine surprise registered on his father's face. Both eyebrows raised toward the ceiling. "Well I'll be. You are one for keeping the *ton* guessing. I take it you have come for money," replied the duke.

Harry shook his head. "No. I have come to give you my news and to ask for your blessing. Nothing more."

Lord Steele nodded toward the door. "Let us go sit in the

formal drawing room. This calls for a more friendly place in which to chat."

They crossed the hallway, headed for the door opposite. The head butler was waiting a little distance away.

The duke waved him over. "Could you please bring us up a pot of strong black tea and some thin toast with anchovy paste?"

Anchovy paste. His father might well have thrown him out of the house, but he still remembered his youngest son's favorite food.

"My son will be staying for refreshments."

My son. How long has it been since you used those words kindly toward me?

The butler smiled and bowed. "Very good, your grace."

They made themselves comfortable in the cozy, warm drawing room. The overstuffed purple floral couches, which his mother preferred to the more formal sofas, had long been some of Harry's favorites. They had been the reason for the big, puffy ones he had purchased for his own home.

"Now, tell me all about this chit," said Lord Steele, settling into his comfy couch.

Alice was many things, but a chit she most certainly was not. The future Lady Harry Steele was a strong young woman.

"Her name is Miss Alice North. Her father deals in textiles and trade," said Harry.

His father's eyes lit with delight. He clasped his hands together loudly and shook them. "Huzzah! Well done, Harry! You've gone and landed yourself an heiress. I didn't think you had it in you, but that's capital news."

Harry waited until his father's gleeful celebration simmered down a touch before replying, "She has a watertight marriage settlement, so there will not be a big fat dowry coming my way. Alice and I will live comfortably on an annual allowance from her father, plus the money I bring in."

"Pfft. Damn new money. They might not have the breeding or titles, but they know their way around a contract," replied his father.

The butler finally reappeared in the doorway bearing a tray, which he set down on the table between the two couches. After pouring both the duke and Harry a cup of tea, he bowed and left, closing the door behind him.

Harry's stomach growled as his nose picked up the spicy aroma of anchovy on warm toast. How long had it been since he had tasted heaven?

"I understand you have established a business of sorts with the Duke of Monsale and some other chaps. It is going to be enough to support you and a family?"

Of course, his father wanted to know how he was going to go for money. The whole question of funds had been the cause of their massive falling out; Harry had refused to take up a respectable but low-paying career just to placate his family.

"The coaching company is still in its infancy, but I have had another money-making venture operating over the past year," he replied.

Lord Steele picked up his steaming black tea and downed a mouthful. How the man could do that and not wince as it burned his tongue Harry had never been able to figure out.

"Yes, I managed to get something of the truth about your peacock act from your mother, not that I approve of dabbling in other people's misfortunes. Though I do have to ask how you expect to keep that going once you have taken on a wife."

The thought had already occurred to Harry. He was not going to be able to flounce into balls and parties garishly dressed when he had Alice on his arm.

"Of course, if you came back to the fold, I could speak to someone about a job for you. Something in a government ministry. Solid, respectable, and money which you could count on."

Harry shuddered. He could never do that—not now not ever. "Alice and I shall manage. You know I couldn't do a ministerial role. Sitting at a desk, pushing paper all day would kill me."

"So, you are determined to remain outside of the family. Is that what you are saying?" replied the duke.

As he and Alice had lain sleepily together in the bed the previous afternoon, Harry had considered what he wanted from seeing his father. Money hadn't even come into the equation.

"I want to be a part of this family again, but it has to be on terms which suit the both of us. Christmas is coming soon, and I don't want a repeat of last year when I spent Christmas Eve getting drunk in a dirty pub instead of sitting down to dine with my parents and family. Can't we just be father and son, and not at each other's throats?"

He picked up a piece of the toast and stuffed it into his mouth, chewing quietly while he waited for a response. If the duke said no, he was no worse off than he had been an hour earlier.

"You know your mother huffs loudly every time our carriage passes the front of your house. She blames me for this schism, says I am too hard on you."

Harry swallowed the toast. "I have to admit to taking some comfort from her telling me that whenever I see her for lunch in town. I am her sweetest little birdy, and you have thrown me out of the nest."

Lord Steele rolled his eyes. "I swear, the pair of you have been sent to try me. But let us set our differences aside and try to be kind to one another. You and your new fiancée are invited to Christmas Eve supper."

Huzzah!

This was a major victory. He didn't consider it a win over his father—rather a step forward for the entire Steele family. He had missed too many celebrations and occasions already.

"Thank you, Papa. I shall speak with Alice and let her know that Christmas Eve is planned."

"Good, and you can also tell her that the two of you will be visiting Redditch Hall for your honeymoon. You still have to deliver Milton number ten to the breeding program. He is now old enough to do the job," said the duke.

"As long as Alice and I can bring Milton number eleven back to London with us," replied Harry. However small that it was, he was keen to maintain his role with the family estate.

But before he and Alice formally announced their betrothal, there was one last major hurdle for him to clear. He had to convince Mister North to amend the marriage settlements so he could have the funds to set up the RR Coaching Company with a new coach and team of horses. That had been Alice's bright idea.

The only way he was going to be able to give Alice the life she deserved, was to give up his scandals business and do his all to make the RR Coaching Company pay its own way.

As he set foot out into Grosvenor Street an hour later, his stomach gently sloshing from tea and toast, Harry stopped and glanced up at the sky. God may not have wanted him for the church, but he clearly still had plans for the life of Lord Harry Steele.

"An honest businessman? This is going to be interesting," he muttered.

He headed homeward, looking forward to a future with Alice—one which would allow the both of them to be free of their cages. One where they could truly be themselves.

Epilogue

Lady Naomi Steele tracked the slow, almost nervous, progress of the Duke of Monsale as he made his way along the aisle of St George's church. She tittered into her hand. Anyone would think he was the chap getting married today, not her brother.

Tall, tawny-haired, and stubborn. Yet from the moment she had first become aware of herself as being a woman, her marital sights had been set on him.

Her mother elbowed her gently in the ribs. "Stop staring, Naomi. It isn't polite."

She gave her mother a tired glance. "The only thing, which is impolite here, is his reluctance to marry," she whispered.

The Duke of Monsale was one and thirty—well past the age when he should have taken on a wife. The man was impossible. Had she mentioned stubborn?

There is only seven years between us—not too much for it to appear out of sorts for us to marry. You just have to give me a chance. Give us a chance. If Harry can marry, then so can you.

Naomi's gaze now settled on her brother. Harry was dressed formally for church but still had his personal flair about him. The silver pig charm which hung from a pocket-watch chain had her smiling. She silently gave her approval of his delightful salmon and silver striped waistcoat. It was wonderful to see him happy and back in the family fold.

Harry was stupidly in love with Alice North, the girl he was about to wed. From what she could gather, Alice's affections were not much different.

Ah, love.

An early-January wedding was perfect timing. It gave the members of the *ton* still in London something to do during the long, boring days after Christmas and New Year's. Though from the way her mother spoke, you would think it was the only event which would matter all the new year.

The minister at the front of the church lifted his hands, and the congregation all rose. Heads turned. The bride and her father began to make their way toward the altar. The bride wore a long cream gown, matched perfectly by one of the Steele family heirloom sapphire tiaras. The smile on Alice's face was more breathtaking than the priceless jewels; Naomi blinked back another tear.

I am going to be a blubbering mess before this is over.

As the bridal procession passed by the Duke of Monsale, he bowed his head. Naomi was pleased he approved of the union.

Now if someone could just get you to start thinking about the need for an heir or two.

His gaze followed the bride, then drifted to the left. It fell on Naomi and lingered. She swallowed deeply, her heart thumping in her chest.

You look magnificent in your black formal attire. But you are stunning in anything.

Andrew McNeal always had this effect on her. Whenever he was near, she found herself reduced to a tongue-tied fool. Even from this distance, she was drawn in by his gray eyes. Those clear pools of lust . . .

You are in a church for heaven's sake. Stop thinking like that!

And then he smiled. A slow, salacious grin appeared on his face. The rogue knew exactly what he was doing to her. And what she would love him to do.

Naomi blinked slowly, then licked her bottom lip.

Two can play at that game.

The Duke of Monsale might well consider himself the King of Rogues, but Lady Naomi Steele was determined that one day she would be his queen.

Turn the page to read the first chapter of the next instalment of the **Rogues of the Road.**

Stolen by the Rogue.

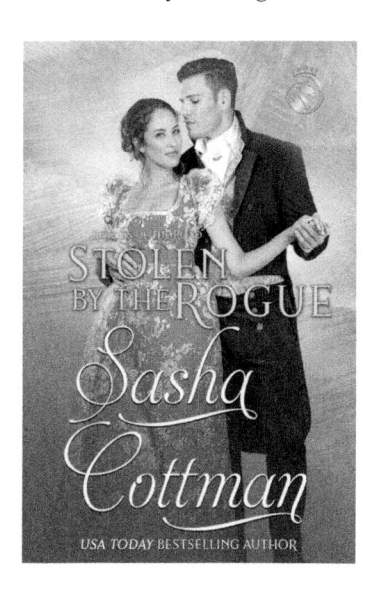

Join my VIP readers and claim your FREE BOOK
A Wild English Rose

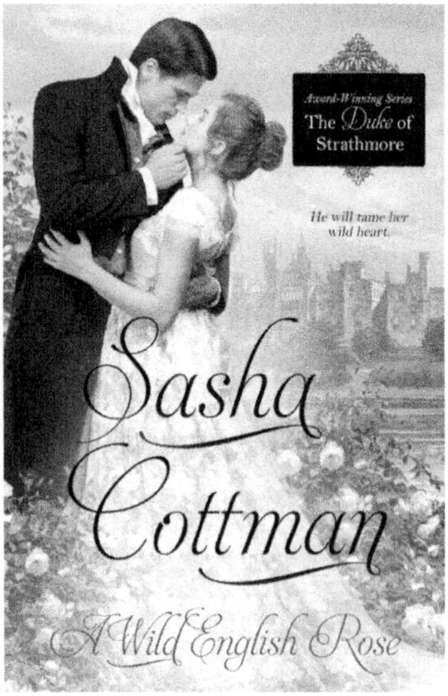
Award-Winning Series
The Duke of Strathmore
He will tame her wild heart.
Sasha Cottman
A Wild English Rose

Stolen by the Rogue

❧

L ondon
  September 1816

George Hawkins silently dropped from the top of the high brick wall and into the rear yard of the art gallery. His leather boots barely made a sound as they hit the ground. Crouching low, he glanced at the night sky and slyly grinned. The dark cover of a new moon was always welcome in his line of work. Tonight, was going to be good; he could feel it in his bones.

His enthusiasm ebbed just a touch as he caught a glimpse of light shining through the window of an upper floor. It was well past nine o'clock; the place should have been empty.

Come on. It's late. Don't you have a tasty supper waiting for you somewhere?

There was nothing worse than an over-efficacious security guard. Such men were the bane of George's career. How was a master thief supposed to get his hands on a lovely piece of lucre if some poorly paid night watchman was too keen to do his job properly?

He shifted to a spot against the wall where it was a little darker and waited. Only a fool would risk taking a chance when an armed sentry was still on patrol. During one of his earlier reconnaissance missions, he had noticed that the guard in question had a pistol poking out from his jacket. Armed security at an art gallery—what was the world coming to?

"About bloody time," he muttered, when the light finally moved away.

He could just picture the man, lantern in hand, methodically checking every exhibition room as he made his way downstairs toward the front door and finally out into Oxford Street.

Good chap. Scuttle off home to your wife.

Not long now and George would have the place all to himself.

Reaching into his coat pocket, he fingered the set of skeleton keys he kept on his person at all times. His father had given them to George as a jest on the occasion of his sixteenth birthday. How a man who sat in judgement of thieves every day at the Old Bailey could find such a thing amusing, George had never been able to fathom. But he had politely accepted the keys and put them to good use almost straight away.

As he had done on many another night, George pushed the thought of his honest magistrate father to the back of his mind and refocused on the job at hand. Being the secret black sheep of the family came with its own price. He couldn't afford to suddenly grow a conscience when he was in the middle of a heist.

George gave it a respectable ten minutes before deciding it was safe to push off the wall and make his way to the back entrance. Still, he wasn't taking any chances, keeping to the shadowy edges of the yard and only coming out into the open when he was close to the rear entry.

A quick dash and he was standing at the door, keys at the ready.

And time for a professional pause.

He took a deep breath, then listened. Craftsmen always measured twice before cutting, while master thieves checked to make certain that they were not going to be disturbed.

Confident that he was indeed alone, George set a key to the lock. He smirked as the first one he chose fitted neatly into the hole and gave a satisfying click as it turned.

Every time, you pick it just right. George Hawkins, you are a clever lad.

Pushing the door open, he froze as the squeak of a tired hinge disturbed the perfect silence of the night. He gritted his teeth.

Bloody hell.

If he were the owner of this building, he would be having a firm word with the person tasked to oil the locks and latches. His heart thumped hard in his chest. At this stage of the operation, any sort of surprise wasn't a welcome one. He waited once more, carefully listening before stepping inside.

George closed the door behind him, wincing as it creaked again. He stilled, allowing his hearing to become accustomed to the little noises that the art gallery made. Buildings were living, breathing organisms with soft symphonies of their own. It took a special kind of mind to notice and understand them.

In order to become a successful criminal, a man had to develop both his hearing and his patience.

When he was certain that he was the only person in the building, George pressed ahead. One foot followed another as he made his way over to the wide oak staircase and began to ascend. Doing his best to ignore his racing heart, he slowly crept on.

Second door on the left. Far wall. Three frames over to the right. No need for a light.

He knew the painting well enough in the daylight, having visited the public showing on several occasions during the proceeding weeks. By attending during the busiest periods, he had been able to conceal himself within the crowded ranks of gallery visitors. It had also given George the chance to watch the guards while remaining out of sight of their prying eyes.

After entering the exhibition space, he crossed the floor then came to a halt in front of the third mounted painting. He stared at it for a time, then softly sighed.

Titian's *Venus with a Mirror* never failed to make him happy.

It was a masterful representation of the goddess, naked while studying herself in a mirror. Titian had reached the pinnacle of his career with the use of rich colors and subject. When he caught a glimpse of Venus's breasts in the dull light, George licked his lips.

Now there was a man who appreciated the naked female form.

And if the masterful work of the artist's brush wasn't enough, the fact that the painting was worth a small fortune was enough of a reason to make a professional thief smile. If George could steal it, and find a willing buyer, all his money problems would be over.

He leaned in close.

Forty-nine inches by forty-one. The perfect size for a one-man mission.

With one hand resting on the top of the frame, the other supporting its weight, he lifted the painting up and away from its mount before setting it gently onto the floor.

BANG!

He whirled round. Someone had slammed the front door. Heavy footsteps echoed on the stairs.

"Bloody ridiculous. Fancy forgetting your dinner tin. She'll have my guts for garters if I come home without it," a low voice chastised.

"Bugger," George muttered.

The potbellied guard had returned. If George remained where he was, the man would pass by the door on the way to the storeroom. He would surely see a night thief, priceless painting at his feet, and all hell would break loose.

Quickly abandoning the Titian, George made for the opposite wall, praying that if the guard did happen to step into the room, he may by some miracle be able to slip out behind the man and leave unnoticed.

The footsteps came closer. George's heart beat hard and fast in his chest. All his worst nightmares were fast becoming reality. A large bead of sweat trickled down his spine.

Back pressed hard against the wall, he inched his way closer to the door, ready to bolt the second the watchman entered the room.

The footsteps stopped a mere yard or so away out in the hall.

"What the devil is going on?" said the man.

Bloody. Bloody. Bollocks.

George waited until his adversary had made it all the way into the room and was standing, hands on rounded hips, looking down at the painting before finally making his move. He took three deft steps to his left and bolted for the door.

"Hey! Stop, thief!"

He leapt down the staircase, dropping with a hard thud onto the first main landing before scurrying for the next set of risers. Footsteps thudded close behind.

A bullet pinged over his head and into the mahogany wood of the wall ahead of him. George didn't stop to count his blessings. Instead, he focused his gaze and prayers solely on the front door.

"Sweet Lord let it be unlocked," he muttered.

If the guard had secured the door behind him when he returned, George was going to be in serious trouble. Fighting his way out of the gallery would be his only option. The sound of the man's footsteps grew louder as he closed the distance between them.

"Come back here, you villain. I'll skin you alive!"

The angry guard was close on his heels when George reached for the handle. He almost wept for joy when it turned, and the door swung open. A gust of cold night air smacked him in the face, but he paid it no mind. Only escape mattered.

He raced out into the street, ignoring the foul curses and loud shouts coming from behind him. No, he wasn't going to stop or come back, thank you very much. With legs pumping and arms swinging, he ran at full stretch along Oxford Street, darting out into the road when other late-night strollers impeded his progress.

At Argyle Street, he made a sharp right turn. The path ahead was clear of pedestrians. Digging deep into what was left of his energy reserves, George increased his pace.

He ran straight past the front door of his home and continued on at breakneck speed, only slowing to take the corner into Great Marlborough Street. After ducking out of sight into the doorway of a shop, he finally came to a skittering halt.

As he bent, hands on knees, and tried to catch his breath, he kept his gaze fixed firmly on the street. To his bone-deep relief, there was no sign of his pursuer.

George panted and wheezed as he sucked in one great lungful of air after the other. The adrenaline coursing through his body made him nauseous. If he hadn't been in the middle of a London street, he would have given in to temptation and cast up his accounts.

Several minutes passed before his heart rate finally returned to normal. His days of being a champion athlete at school and the resultant muscle memory had saved him tonight, but it had been a near-run thing. His fitness wasn't anywhere near as good as it had once been.

Thank God that guard couldn't fire a pistol to save himself, let alone stop an art thief.

In all his years of thieving and smuggling, he had never come this close to being caught. Or shot.

I must have missed something or not waited long enough. Heavens, am I losing my touch?

After a quick wipe of his face with a handkerchief, George straightened his attire and made ready to go home. There was little point in wasting any more time standing out in the street. All his careful planning and preparation had come to naught. The Titian would never be his.

You escaped with your life. Be grateful for that large blessing.

He checked at the corner of Argyle Street and found it was clear. The overweight and unfit guard hadn't been able to keep up with him.

That was too bloody close for anyone's liking. What if he had been a better shot? I might well be dead.

He took in a deep, calming breath and straightened his shoulders.

By the time George Hawkins reached his home at number 45 Argyle Street, his pace had dropped to that of a leisurely saunter.

Only a fool would come tearing in the front door of his father's house as if the hounds of hell were hot on his tail.

He nodded at the footman who answered the door, giving him a friendly grin as he stepped inside. But George's self-assured smile froze on his lips when his gaze settled on the crowd of people who were gathered in the foyer and main ballroom of the Hawkins family home.

Everywhere he looked there was a senior member of the London judiciary. Magistrates, barristers, and even a smattering of King's Counsels stood shoulder to shoulder, drinking and laughing.

Hell, and the devil. I forgot the legal soiree was on tonight.

The sick, heavy feeling in the pit of his stomach returned.

If things had not gone his way just a few minutes earlier, he may well have found himself being hauled up in front of one of his father's friends and made to face judgement.

And I would have been found guilty.

His mother appeared from out of the crowd. She took one look at him, frowned, and hurried to his side. "George, my sweet boy, you don't look at all well. Are you coming down with something?"

"No, I just . . ."

Before he could stop her, Mrs. Hawkins had placed a hand on George's brow. She shook her head and tutted. "Definitely warm and a little sweaty. Maybe you should head upstairs to bed. An early night might be in order. Just remember I am having Lady Dodd and her daughter, Petunia, over tomorrow afternoon, and you did promise to stop by and give them your regards."

Not another matchmaking attempt, Mama. Please. I don't need you to find me a wife.

"Perhaps I should make it an early night. Though if I am still not right in the morning, you may have to give Lady Dodd my sincere apologies," he replied.

Anything he did to avoid having to take tea and cake with yet another young miss on his mother's ever-growing list of potential brides was worth it. A good son shouldn't lie to his mother about being ill, but George had told so many untruths to his parents over the years that they rolled off his tongue without a second thought.

I really am the worst of the family.

He was about to make good on his promise to head upstairs when the Honorable Judge Hawkins hailed him from the doorway of the ballroom. "Ah! George, I was wondering if you were going to make it home in time for my little gathering. Good to see you, son." He hurried over.

Mrs. Hawkins turned to her husband. "I think George is unwell. I suggested he should turn in."

The look of disappointment on his father's face put a swift end to George's plans for a speedy exit. He hadn't done the expected thing and followed his father and brother into the legal fraternity. And while Judge Hawkins made obvious attempts to hide his feelings, it was clear to George that his sire still hadn't come to terms with his youngest son's rejection of the family calling.

"I am certain I could manage one drink," replied George.

His father's demeanor changed in an instant. "Excellent. Grab a glass and come and say a quick hello to the Lord High Chancellor. Lord Eldon was just about to tell us the story of a wicked jewel thief they executed at Newgate Prison this morning. I am sure you will find it fascinating."

If caught, I would have been sentenced. And I would have been hung.

A reluctant George took a brandy from a footman and followed his father into the ballroom. He could just imagine how it would feel to be a condemned man taking his final steps on the way to the scaffold.

That could've been me.

"Lord Eldon, you remember my son George, don't you?" said his father.

George stirred from his horrid imaginings of death and bowed low. "My lord."

As he righted himself, his gaze met that of the man who, aside from the King, was the most powerful legal authority in all of England—a man who one day could very well hold George's fate in his hands. It wouldn't matter if he was the son of a judge; he would not be shown any mercy.

He swallowed deeply as grey, all-seeing eyes stared back at him. And in that moment, George Hawkins made a fateful decision.

I have to find another way to make money or I am destined to end up swinging by my neck at the end of a rope. I must give up this life of villainy. But how?

. . .

Continue reading **Stolen by the Rogue**

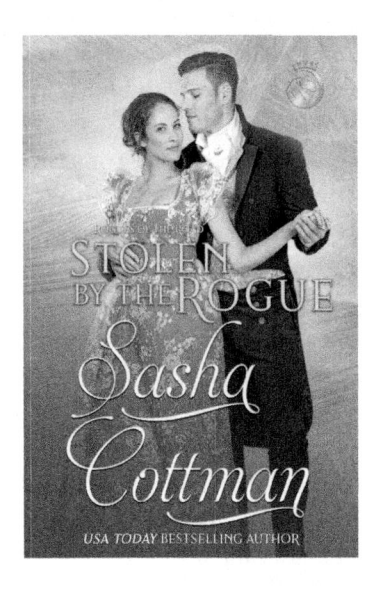

Stolen by the Rogue

A king's secret mistress. A master thief in search of a priceless treasure. One woman holds the key to it all.

The Honorable George Hawkins is a man caught between two worlds. On one hand he is the respectable son of a senior London judge, on the other he is a founding member of the dirty-dealing, Rogues of the Road.

On the hunt for ancient gold he meets antiquities expert Jane Scott and is immediately smitten. George decides that there is nothing better than mixing business with pleasure and sets his sights on wooing Jane.

And while Jane is no fool and sees right through George's plan, her heart is still determined to win his love.

An old letter written in cypher sends the two lovers on the

trail of a great, secret prize. A king's treasure of gold and jewels.

But with every step on the path to discovery, both Jane and George find themselves wondering whether they can trust the other. Will love, have to be the price they both pay in order to succeed?

Stolen by the Rogue.

Also by Sasha Cottman

SERIES

The Kembal Family
The Duke of Strathmore
The Noble Lords
Rogues of the Road
London Lords

The Kembal Family

Tempted by the English Marquis

The Vagabond Viscount

The Duke of Spice

The Duke of Strathmore

Letter from a Rake

An Unsuitable Match

The Duke's Daughter

A Scottish Duke for Christmas

My Gentleman Spy

Lord of Mischief

The Ice Queen

Two of a Kind

A Lady's Heart Deceived

All is Fair in Love

Duke of Strathmore Novellas

Mistletoe and Kisses
Christmas with the Duke
A Wild English Rose

The Noble Lords

Love Lessons for the Viscount
A Lord with Wicked Intentions
A Scandalous Rogue for Lady Eliza
Unexpected Duke
The Noble Lords Boxed Set

Rogues of the Road

Rogue for Hire
Stolen by the Rogue
When a Rogue Falls
The Rogue and the Jewel
King of Rogues
The Rogues of the Road Boxed Set

London Lords

Devoted to the Spanish Duke
Promised to the Swedish Prince
Seduced by the Italian Count
Wedded to the Welsh Baron
Bound to the Belgian Count

USA Today bestselling author Sasha Cottman's novels are set around the Regency period in England, Scotland, and Europe. Her books are centred on the themes of love, honor, and family.

www.sashacottman.com

Facebook
Instagram
TikTok
Join my VIP readers and claim your FREE BOOK
A Wild English Rose

Writing as Jessica Gregory

Jessica Gregory
SASSY STEAMY ROMANCE

Jessica Gregory writes sassy steamy rom coms. She loves strong heroines and making her heroes grovel.

Royal Resorts

Room for Improvement

A Suite Temptation

The Last Resort

Sign up for Planet Billionaire and receive your FREE BOOK.

An Italian Villa Escape